HARMONY GLEN
COZY MONSTER ROMANCE

A TROLL IN THE HAY

KARLA DOYLE

Contents

A Troll in the Hay

a sweet-and-spicy cozy monster romance

OGRAM

Trolls are notoriously solitary, and though I long to find my one true mate, life on my farm, surrounded by earth and crops, has always been enough to fulfill me.

Until the day Hope walks into my farm market to purchase a basket of apples. From that moment, all I can think about is filling *her* basket. Making her mine for the rest of our days.

But Hope is only in Harmony Glen on holiday, meaning I have limited time to make the woman who's never dated a monster fall in love with my big, green, tusk-toothed troll self...or lose what my heart knows is my one chance at love.

HOPE

After monsters stepped out of the shadows, I learned my hometown community isn't just small-minded, *they're* the true monsters.

So, I squirreled away my waitressing tips until I had saved enough for a vacation in Harmony Glen, a small town in Upstate New York known for its "harmonious" multispecies integration. My plan was to see and meet as many monsters as possible, so I could go back home and tell everyone how wrong they are to vilify nonhumans.

What I wasn't counting on? Falling instantly head over heels for a seven-foot-tall troll when I walk into his charming farm market store.

Ogram is quiet and reclusive. I'm the opposite. It shouldn't work, but it does. It really, *really* does.

Should I chalk it up to the best vacation ever and leave with once-in-a-lifetime memories, or stay and build a forever life with the only person who's ever felt like home?

A Troll in the Hay is a short, sweet, fluffy, spicy fated mates/instalove story set in the Harmony Glen world. Expect over-the-top instant mutual attraction, humorous language gaffes, size difference, and a troll whose sweetness is only rivaled by the spice he brings.

Map of Harmony Glen

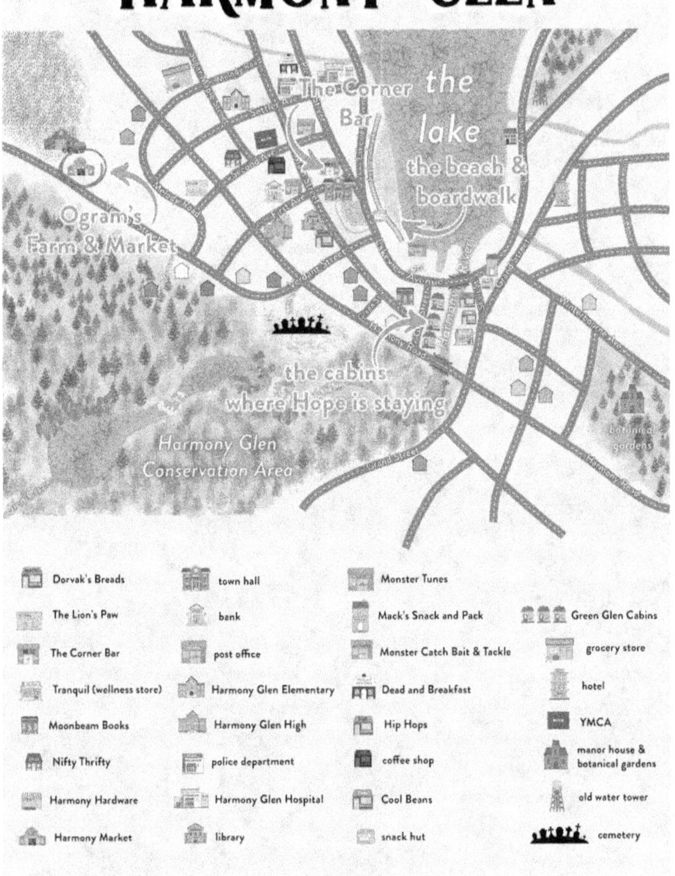

Chapter One

OGRAM

"We don't see you in here often," Mrs. Mitchell says as I ring up her purchases on the market's cash register. "Getting to work indoors must be a nice change from being out in the fields."

With painstaking care, I tap in the last of her items. None of my employees who work in the market store have ever complained about the cash register's buttons being too small, but like many things in the human-dominated world, this equipment wasn't designed for use by someone my size. With my thick fingers, it's a miracle I'm even able to tap a single key, let alone with any accuracy.

Being temporarily short an employee, I don't have much choice. But it's not the *nice change* my well-meaning, gray-haired human customer suggested. I'm a troll. A creature of nature. Being outside among the earth and plants has always been my peace, my comfort. I'd be happy to leave the store duties to my employees indefinitely.

But that's not what she wants to hear, and despite preferring solitude to socializing, I never want to be impolite to anyone. "Spending time in the store is an opportunity to say hello to the many fine people who honor me by shopping here." I finish with the expression I've practiced in front of a mirror to soften the effect my large tusks can have on a smile. I gather the squash, zucchini, onions, greens and apples into her cloth shopping bags while Mrs. Mitchell places her cash on the counter, all of it coins, stacked in tidy piles.

She's the fifth person to pay by cash today. Cash means I don't have to fiddle with the even tinier buttons on the electronic payment terminal, but it also means I'll have to go downtown to the bank, and during business hours, no less, since her contribution to the cash deposit is akin to a leprechaun's bag of treasure. Downtown has a lot more people than the customers at my market store, even on its busiest day. The thought of all the required face-to-face interaction sends a shiver down my spine.

Mrs. Mitchell snaps her coin purse closed and smiles at me. "Well, I hope you'll take this opportunity among people to do more than say hello. A fellow like you should have someone special waiting after a long day's work, not go home to an empty farmhouse. You know, I could bring my granddaughter by for you to meet. Gertrude would make a wonderful wife for someone like you."

As much as the humans of Harmony Glen have

welcomed other species with open arms since the Great Revelation, I doubt her "someone like you" means a keeps-to-himself, hardworking farmer. More likely: a big, brutish-looking, borderline-reclusive monster with zero romantic prospects but above-adequate financial resources. Someone who'd be grateful for any match. Regardless of her motivation, she's open-minded enough to suggest a union between our species, and that's not small potatoes.

"I'm honored you'd consider introducing me to your granddaughter, but I must decline."

"Oh?" Mrs. Mitchell's eyebrows shoot upward, chasing the lines of her forehead beneath a row of tight silver curls held snugly in place by a bright-purple hair scarf. "I hadn't heard any whispers around town that you'd become romantically attached to someone. Who is it?"

There's no one, but I should lie and say there is. I'd rather not tell her the reason I declined has nothing to do with being involved with someone else, and everything to do with the size of my cock. Physical intimacy with other species isn't impossible, but taking my girth would be a challenge for a human woman, requiring preparation many would find...objectionable. Especially for a single, casual instance of gratification, which is all I could offer anyone who is not my mate.

Mrs. Mitchell must take my hesitation to provide a name as an unspoken confirmation that I'm still romantically unattached, because her eyebrows return to their normal position and a smile crests her lips. "Will you be in the store for the rest of the afternoon? I'll fetch my sweet Gertie and come back at closing time so you won't be interrupted by customers. She's quiet, much in the way you are, and very innocent. I'm sure you'll be immediately smitten."

My jaw clenches so tightly I wouldn't be surprised if Mrs. Mitchell can hear my back teeth grinding. If she knew anything about troll mating urges, she wouldn't want me to be immediately smitten with her sweet, innocent granddaughter. Luckily for Gertrude, I'm sure that won't happen. I've met many human women since Harmony Glen welcomed monsters to integrate in the community, and I've never experienced even a twinge of desire toward any.

With few female trolls residing in the area and none of them sparking something inside me, it's likely I'll spend my life alone. Many trolls do. As much as I'd like to find a mate—solitude, safety, and working the land make a good life.

"I'm sure anyone would be lucky to be married to your granddaughter, but I spend most of my waking hours working on the farm, so I wouldn't be the husband your granddaughter deserves. But if she's looking for a part-time job, I'm still searching for someone to take this spot in the market store, so I can get back to the fields full time."

Given the way Mrs. Mitchell's mouth thins to a downward curve, I'd guess she doesn't care for what I thought to be a respectful and tactful answer.

"She needs a husband, not an employer. Good day to

you, Ogram," she says, turning away with her chin tilted high, nearly bumping an incoming customer while huffing a dramatic exit.

I don't owe an apology to the woman who quickly skips sideways to avoid being jostled by the obviously disgruntled matchmaker. Even if I wanted to be courteous and call out a friendly, "Sorry about that," I can't, because my mouth goes dry and my insides grow tight and hot and electrified when my gaze connects with the human's as she moves deeper into the store.

She's beautiful. The loveliest creature I've ever laid eyes on. Fair skin with a rosy tint, long hair that looks like dark-brown silk, and hourglass curves. The sunlight streaming through the open roll-up door behind her gives her an angelic glow.

Moving around the tables of produce, she doesn't stop to look at any of it. Not a single glance, even as she scoops a small basket of apples from one of the tables she passes. Her focus remains on me, drifting from my eyes to my tall, pointed ears poking through my shaggy, shoulder-length hair, to the long tusks protruding from my lower gums that reach nearly to my cheekbones. My most monstrous features. That she can see, anyway.

The other monstrous part of me is thick and hard against my left thigh, threatening to break the inner seam of my work pants. I've never had this kind of physical reaction to a human.

And it's not just my cock responding. Every step she takes toward me amplifies the tingling sensation running rampant through my body. My heart thumps so wildly, I wouldn't be surprised if she can see it pounding against my green skin in the V where my shirt is unbuttoned.

As long as she doesn't see the bulge filling out my pant leg. Which she won't because I'm essentially frozen in place behind the counter. Like a deer trapped in the headlights. Only it's not a collision and death that's imminent, it feels like the opposite. As if I'm waking up fully for the first time, or seeing a whole range of colors I didn't know existed until this moment.

"Hi," she says, placing the basket, then both palms, on the smooth wood countertop separating us. Her hands are so much smaller than mine. Her fingers, so delicate.

"Just the apples today?" Miraculously, my voice works. And my brain, enough to form that simple yet coherent question.

"I apologize for staring." The apple question goes unanswered as she blinks up at me. A gentle head shake causes her hair to move like dark waves against the pale shores of her bare shoulders. "I'm visiting town, and where I'm from, there's been very little integration since the Great Revelation. You're the first orc I've ever seen in person."

Trolls generally bristle at being mistaken for orcs. This woman could mistake me for a sentient cactus and I wouldn't get prickly. Still, I'd be a negligent representative of nonhumans if I didn't educate her about the different species.

"Welcome to Harmony Glen," I say with a nod and one of my carefully practiced smiles. "I'm not at all bothered by your attention, so please, stare all you like. One detail though—I'm a troll, not an orc."

An adorable squeak leaves her lips before her hands fly up to cover her face. "I'm sorry! You must think I'm the dumbest, most oblivious human ever." The mumbled words are easy to distinguish, even from behind her self-imposed muzzle.

She doesn't know that trolls have excellent hearing, and I'm not about to tell her. Not yet.

"Could you say that again, but without the..." I make a sweep-away motion toward my own mouth.

She drops her hands from their screening position, revealing cheeks I'd very much like to reach across and touch, to see if their increased shade of pink is just a pretty color, or if the tint has affected the temperature of her skin. "I'm so sorry for assuming. It's just that you're very big, and you're green, and you have those protruding bottom teeth." Again, she shakes her head. "I've seen a lot of media coverage about orcs since the beginning of multispecies integration, but I don't recall seeing anything about trolls, and in my mind, trolls are small and —" Her lips snap closed, her complexion developing an even deeper blush.

When she doesn't finish the abruptly cut-off sentence, I motion for her to continue. "Small and..."

Something between a sigh and an agonized groan leaves her lips as she looks up at me through long, dark eyelashes. "Creepy and ugly—and before you think the worst of me, which I don't blame you for—I want you to know that *I* think the worst of me right now. I feel horrible about having unflattering preconceived notions about any species. Especially yours, after meeting you. You're the opposite of all those things I so wrongly assumed."

Even if I wasn't unexpectedly and utterly attracted to her, I'd find her earnestness charming. "Yes, I'm definitely the opposite of small," I say, addressing the only point it's reasonable to believe she meant genuinely. "Don't be hard on yourself for the assumptions. Trolls are generally quite solitary in nature, and our preference to avoid public and social gatherings means there isn't a lot of accurate information about us available, even since integration with human communities."

"You're very kind, forgiving me so easily."

"There's nothing to forgive. You made a minor, honest mistake; don't give it another thought. Now that that's out of the way, if you have any questions about trolls or Harmony Glen, please feel free to ask. I'm happy to help you any way I can." Though my customer probably doesn't consider this a personal conversation, I'd like it to be. I don't want the interaction to end. I don't want her to turn around and walk out of the market. Out of my life.

Placing her hands on the counter again, she slides them toward my side. An innocent action that causes my already indecent reaction to her to expand. Then she leans in, essentially putting her breasts on the countertop.

Towering over as I do, I have a clear view down the neckline front of her formfitting summer dress, and my gaze is drawn to the deep valley between her smooth, rounded breasts. My cock throbs against my leg, and a trickle of precum slides down my skin. I can't recall the last time I took myself in hand for a release, but I know when the next time will be—as soon as the farmhouse door is closed behind me tonight. And I'll be picturing this beautiful human with every stroke and spurt.

"Okay, I have a question," she says, smiling when my gaze snaps from her breasts to her waiting eyes. Green, a shade much like my skin. They're also glittering, and since there's no sunlight directly shining on this part of the store, the sparkle must be coming from within.

"Of course. Ask me anything."

"Was your offer of help just generic politeness that you hope I don't take you up on? You know, given what you said about being antisocial." For a human woman who has no experience with trolls, and comes from somewhere without much monster integration, she's incredibly forward and fearless.

"Any offer I make to you is sincere."

Delicate dark eyebrows rise over her dazzling green eyes. Did she take note of my carefully worded *to you*? Was my desperation for her to accept obvious?

Her lips part as if to respond, but anything she might've said is interrupted by voices and laughter as a family with several young children enters, pulling a wagon laden with baskets from the pick-your-own fields.

"Hi, Mr. Ogram!" one of the littles calls out, waving a long carrot with its top intact while running toward me. "Look what I picked!"

The dark-haired beauty eases back from the counter. "I'll get out of your way, *Mr. Ogram.*"

"Just Ogram," I say as she moves aside to make space for the incoming miniature tornado. "And you're not in the way. I'll just be a few minutes taking care of these folks, then I'm all yours if you'd like to take me up on that offer."

The smile she gives me nearly buckles my knees. "I absolutely do. I'm Hope, by the way."

Hope. She couldn't have a more perfect name.

Chapter Two

HOPE

Since arriving in Harmony Glen several days ago, I've seen so many monsters of all shapes and sizes. The first day I was exploring downtown, a lion man walked by with what looked like a baby dragon. It was very difficult not to stare, but if he noticed, he didn't seem bothered. Neither did the blue-skinned man who appeared ready to stop and talk as if we're friends when I said hello in passing. And that was just the first afternoon. Everyone I've met has been welcoming, if not honest-to-goodness delightful.

Like I told Ogram, my hometown didn't embrace multispecies integration after the Great Revelation, when all the nonhuman species came out of hiding. They didn't actually ban monsters from my town, but as soon as the first business hung a "Humans Only" sign, a big chunk of the others quickly followed suit. I thought that eventually the closed-mindedness would end. That the town I'd spent my entire life in would come around and at least *accept* monsters, even if they didn't actively welcome them.

Nope. And it didn't stop with blatant speciesism. Town council became an angry, pitchfork-wielding mob. Okay, fine, there were no pitchforks, and it wasn't a mob so much as a handful of ignorant jerks, but still. They forced one of the longtime resident families out of their home after learning the Wolferds had more *wolf* in them than just their name—they're all wolf shifters. And it's not as if town council unearthed their secret. The Wolferds outed themselves via an interview with *Monster Life* magazine. They've always been nice people and, according to the article, they've never caused any harm to humans while in their wolf form.

Even town council didn't dispute that, and I'm sure if they had even a shred of flimsy evidence, they would've slapped that card down on the table. But they didn't try to pin anything on the Wolferds. They just booted them out of their home for no reason other than their nonhuman status, under the guise of expropriation. Such bullshit.

It's been five years since the Great Revelation. The Wolferds shouldn't have to hide their heritage and true identity. The magazine article was genuine and heart-warming, and should've hit their fellow townsfolk—*my fellow townsfolk*—in the feels. When it did the opposite, and they were borderline-forcibly ousted from the home that'd been in their family for generations, I had to get out of there, even if only for a week and a bit. All I can afford on a waitress's wage in a town where most people are as stingy with their tips as they are with their open-mindedness.

So here I am, in one *Monster Life*'s "Ten Monster-Inclusive Destinations You Won't Want to Miss This Summer" and yes, I did make sure to tell every bigoted person I know where I was taking my vacation and spending those hard-earned tips they gave me. Since my boss was one of those bigots, I may need to find a new job when I go back. If he fires me for being openly pro-integration, he can stuff my uniform apron up his prejudiced ass.

That's a post-vacation problem. No more thinking about the miserable, tight-sphincter town I'm from while I'm here in happy Harmony Glen.

According to the magazine article, even before Harmony Glen gained notice for welcoming all species with open arms, it had a reputation as a charming summer tourist destination. Nestled at the bottom of one of the Finger Lakes, it has lots of quaint shops and restaurants, a variety of water activities at the lake, and a breathtakingly beautiful and expansive conservation area on the outskirts of town.

Those last two things are still on my to-do list. The downtown is so cute, bustling with humans and monsters living and working in unison... it's perfect. I've always loved being surrounded by people, and being immersed in this community, even as a tourist, is like being plugged in to the best kind of energy. That's where I'd be again right now if the owner of the cabins where I'm staying hadn't convinced me to come out to the farm market.

Glen, the owner of the alcove of small rental cabins along the river, was tending the already immaculate grounds when I stepped out of my cabin. He's a tree-man with what looks like woody bark for skin and green vines and leaves for hair. I'll admit to being a little unnerved when I first met him. He's one of many monsters I didn't know existed until I got here. Like everyone else in town, he's been nothing but welcoming and friendly. And adamant that I change my plans for more downtown shopping and head for the farm market instead. *Today*. It had to be today.

When I overhear the family with the energetic children and wagon of freshly picked produce talking to Ogram about how nice it is to find him working in the store for a change, I understand Glen's insistence that I alter my plans.

In our few brief chats, I've told Glen how excited I am to experience a fully integrated community, and my hopes of meeting as many nonhuman species as possible while I'm here. So, it's kind of odd that Glen didn't come out and tell me this might be my only chance to meet a troll, but that doesn't matter, I'm just glad I did. And not so I can add "troll" to a list. Because I met Ogram.

The moment I stepped into this building and our eyes met, something happened. To me anyway, though I swear I felt vibes coming from him during our conversation. Everything about Ogram hits the right notes. He's beyond tall. Broad. Thick. With eyes that twinkle like dark gemstones. Massive hands that could crush me, yet I know, somehow, would be gentle if he touched me. Then there's his mouth.

I want to look at all of him, but my attention keeps drifting to his mouth, my imagination running wild as I picture what it would be like to kiss him. Would his tusks be rough or smooth against my cheeks? Are they sensitive? Would he like it if I touched them? Kissed them? Ran my tongue up and down them? If it turned him on, then what? He's humanlike in many ways—arms, legs, hands, a face with eyes, nose and mouth. Does the similarity continue between his legs? And if he does have a cock, is *it* larger than human size, too?

Heat winds its way through me at the thought of exploring his massive green body. Of having him explore mine. I shift on my feet, squeezing my thighs together and subtly swaying my hips in an attempt to get some pressure on my clit, though that might only make things worse since I'm basically edging myself. To make matters worse, the motion causes my sundress to graze my braless nipples, the combination of sensations requiring I bite my lip to suppress the sexually frustrated groan building in the back of my throat.

In a blink, Ogram's attention swings from the customers at the counter to me. Eyes locked with mine, his chest expands and his nostrils flare.

Fire licks at my cheeks, and I turn away, focusing on a table full of potatoes in various sizes of baskets as if they're the most interesting thing in the world.

Even after the family has said their goodbyes and

exited the store, Ogram still doesn't come over or speak to me from behind the counter. He doesn't even clear his throat. The only sounds in the small space come from outside—muted, fading voices, the crunch of tires on gravel, then birdsong and the hum of cicadas, carried inside on a gentle summer afternoon's breeze. But I know he's still there. I feel his eyes on me.

At some point, I have to turn around. Face him. What's my excuse for staring at him going to be this time? The truth is a bit much to lay on a total stranger, especially one from a species I know nothing about. But lying, pretending I'm not wildly attracted to him, feels wrong. Plus, I'm really not wired for anything other than straightforward telling it like it is. A character flaw, according to pretty much everyone back home.

His deep voiced, "If you thought of any questions, or still want my help ..." slides into my ears as I'm turning toward him.

"I did and I do."

Large hands planted on the wooden countertop in front of him, he gives a single nod. "Then I'm glad to be at your service."

Would he say that if he knew all the ways I've imagined him *servicing* me since laying eyes on him? It's not like I have a monster fetish. I came here for the experience of meeting as many nonhumans as possible and seeing what it's like to be part of a friendly, multispecies community, so I could go back home and tell all the assholes there to stop vilifying nonhumans. At no point did I even *think* about getting involved with someone on this vacation trip. Fucking a monster isn't some freaky bucket-list item I want to check off.

But I do want to fuck *him.*

I think.

I'm pretty sure.

Like, ninety-nine percent.

Okay, I'm lying. There is no remaining one percent.

"You said I could ask if I have questions about trolls," I say, moving toward him. "Can it be a personal question?"

His posture stiffens and his mouth becomes a straight line, as much as that's possible with two big tusk teeth protruding from the lower side. His thick russet eyebrows lower over dark eyes that never leave my face. "I..." One hand goes to the back of his neck, rubbing it as if he's trying to unscrew his head. Rosy red blooms across the upper portion of his cheeks, like apples ripening right before my eyes. He has to be at least seven feet tall and wider than a linebacker with pads on, yet he's adorable.

Normally, I'd draw out his agony in the name of flirting. But all I know about trolls is that I want to know more about this one. Right now, simple and direct is probably the safe route. "I wondered if you're romantically involved with anyone, and if you're not, if you'd like to meet me later. Yesterday, I walked past a pub that looked like a fun place, and the sign out front said there's live music on weekends, and tonight it's a spider man. Not like the comic book superhero. A spider who's a man. But you probably already knew that. Or know him."

"I did and I do. You're talking about The Corner Bar."

"That's the one." Smiling, I wait for him to continue. Surely if he were going to decline, he wouldn't have bothered to confirm the location. But instead of answering my key questions, he just stands there looking...pained. Leaving me to do the letting-off-the-hook thing. "Sorry if I put you in an awkward spot with my invitation. Even if you're not attached to someone else, you can say no to me."

"I would prefer not to say no to you."

"There's a silent 'but' at the end of that sentence, I think."

A heavy sigh leaves his mouth, the kind that would make any normal-sized person's shoulders sag. "But I am not at my best in a crowd, and The Corner Bar will be especially busy because of the live music."

"Of course," I say, heaving a sigh of my own. "Not five minutes ago you told me you prefer to avoid public and social events, so what do I do? Invite you to a bar. Duh. If you didn't think I was oblivious before, I'm sure you must now."

"I don't think that at all. I told you trolls are generally of that nature, but I didn't say all trolls are. My brother, for example, doesn't fit the description. He's a rock musician, currently on a North American tour. Unfortunately, I have a typical troll's aversion to socializing."

"You seem to be doing pretty well right now," I say, leaning against the counter and smiling up at him.

"If I am, it's because I don't want our conversation to end."

Is the big, antisocial troll flirting with me? I think he might be. I hope he is.

"If you'd welcome my company after your evening at the pub, it would be my honor and pleasure to see you safely to your accommodations, and perhaps we could talk while we walk."

Yup, now I'm ninety-five percent sure he's interested. Time to get that final five out of the way. "Would we be talking about your girlfriend or wife or other significant person?"

"No, as I have none of those."

Internal fist pump? Heck, yes! "Then, what if I save my pub outing for another night, and we take a longer walk together instead? Maybe along the boardwalk—or if there are too many people there, you could suggest somewhere else. I really haven't seen much of Harmony Glen yet, but I want to experience it all."

"I would like that very much, and the beach will be picturesque in the evening. May I call on you around seven?"

May I call on you, not *pick you up*. Either he's just very polite and formal, or it's been a while since he took someone on a date. Like, a long while. Then again, I have no idea how old he is. I've read that some nonhuman species have much longer lifespans. Regardless, my answer is the same.

"Seven is perfect. I'm staying at the Green Glen Cabins. Number three."

His eyes twinkle as his deep-green lips pull into a smile. "I am very much looking forward to seeing you again."

"Me too." Pretty sure my feet barely touch the ground on my way out. It's only after I've figuratively floated all the way to my car that I realize I left the apples on the counter and didn't buy a single other thing in his farm market. But I left with a date, and no amount of farm-fresh goods could top that.

Chapter Three

HOPE

Being a waitress means I'm a big fan of sensible shoes. That's what I packed, since I planned to do lots of walking around town on this trip, and it's what I *should* wear tonight.

Instead, I went downtown after leaving Harmony Market, poked around several of the charming shops and bought a pair of glossy candy-apple-red peep-toe pumps that are going to kill my feet after about ten minutes of walking. That's probably too generous, honestly. But they're *so* pretty. Infinitely sexier than my comfortable canvas flats with the memory foam insoles.

As usual, I'm ready early. A habit after years of being called in to work ahead of my scheduled start time because some coworker is a last-minute no-show. When my boss calls, it's never actually a request to come in early. It's an expectation that never comes with appreciation.

Hence, why I'm pacing the little cabin with twenty minutes to go until Ogram is due to arrive.

Through the window, I spot Glen, the cabins' owner, in the yard, in front of the inground pool. He's humanlike in some ways—arms with hands, a face with two eyes, a nose, and a mouth. But he's definitely treelike, and there are enough small vines and leaves sprouting on him for me to assume he doesn't just *look* like he has bark for skin, that's what it actually is.

After putting my foot in my mouth with Ogram and incorrectly calling him an orc, I'm not going to ask Glen about his bark skin. Or would it be skin bark? Either way, my curiosity is staying locked down. Some casual conversation should be safe, though. Talking always makes time pass faster, and I'm going to be back in my sensible shoes before Ogram even gets here if I don't stop pacing the cabin.

Grabbing my purse from the chair, I step outside, then make my way across the lawn to join Glen where he's filling an assortment of bird feeders under the canopy of a large katsura tree. Just like the first time I spoke with Glen out here, the tree is giving off a scent that reminds me of pancake breakfasts when I was a little kid.

"Does this tree smell this good all the time?" I ask, breathing it in as I smile at the tall tree-man.

"It is wonderful, isn't it?" Finished pouring black oil sunflower seeds into one of the feeders, Glen carefully closes the bag and sets it aside. "My senses are different from yours, but most horticultural journals state the scent is strongest later in the summer, before the leaves drop."

"Then I guess I chose the perfect time for a visit."

"Every day in Harmony Glen is a perfect day to be here," he says, picking up another variety of birdseed and filling an adorable wooden feeder that looks very much like him, minus the green vines growing from the top of his head. "Did you make it over to Harmony Market?"

"I did, and I figured out why you were so insistent that I go today. You knew Ogram isn't always in the market store, but he would be there today, giving me an opportunity to meet a troll."

Using the same seed mix, he moves on to the next feeder in need of a top-up. "How did it go?"

Heat ripples through me. I don't need to be in front of a mirror to know my cheeks are now bright pink, and from the way the thick ridge above Glen's eyes rises, I'm sure a verbal answer isn't required. Nor do I have an opportunity to give one because the subject of our conversation pulls into the small parking lot, his hulking green form taking up nearly all the space in the front seat of a large pickup truck's cab.

He's early. By fifteen minutes.

Glen turns toward the truck. He raises his free hand in a neighborly gesture, then returns his attention to me. "I assume Ogram's presence here this evening means things went well between the two of you?"

"He was very kind and accommodating. We're going for a walk, probably along the boardwalk at the beach."

"That's more than being kind and accommodating."

Meeting Ogram's gaze across the property sends a ripple of warm tingles through me. Still, this being totally new ground for me, a little reassurance wouldn't hurt. "What makes you think that?" I ask Glen as I gesture for Ogram to join us. I would've expected Glen's laugh to be rough, to match his exterior, but when he chuckles, it's soft and gentle.

"Trolls don't tend to be social creatures. I've known Ogram many years, since before the Revelation. He doesn't venture into town unless it's out of necessity." Glen tips his head subtly in Ogram's direction, where he approaching with a bouquet in one large green hand and two paper bags in the other. "Until now, that is."

My heart feels as if it's doing the hundred-meter dash in my chest.

Denim molds to Ogram's long, thick legs as he walks toward us. His eyes don't waver from mine until he reaches us, and even then, he spares my short-term land-lord only a momentary glance while greeting him. "Evening, Glen."

"Good to see you." Despite four bird feeders being empty or darn close to it, Glen gathers the birdseed bags in both hands, gives each of us a nod, then makes his way to the building which serves as the office, and possibly his residence, though who knows with a man who's also a tree.

Even though Ogram and I are outside and any number of people could be watching from the cabins surrounding us, being alone with him makes it feel as if the world has shrunk to include only the two of us. Bird-song and crickets' chirping are distant sounds compared to my pulse in my ears.

He seems even bigger than when I met him earlier. Without the wooden counter separating us, I legitimately have to tilt my head back to get a proper look at his face. "Hi."

"I'm early," he says, his fingers flexing where he grips the stems of the bouquet.

"I'm glad."

Some of the tension eases from his expression. "These are from my garden at the farmhouse," he says, offering me the bundle of purple flowers with long, thin petals and yellow centers, the stems wrapped in brown kraft paper and tied with twine.

Our fingers touch as he transfers the bouquet to my hands. An innocent brushing of skin that my body responds to in a far from innocent way. My nipples tighten and my clit tingles as if I've been working myself up during the spicy part of a one-handed read. "Thank you, they're so pretty. All those fields of crops and a flower garden too? You really have a green thumb."

"Two of them, in fact," he says, his eyes twinkling as he smiles at me. "But yes, trolls of my kind have a special affinity with the earth and its bounty." He sets one of the bags on the ground, then offers the other before I can ask any of the multiplying questions his comment ignites in my curious brain. "That is not part of the gift." He motions toward the bag on the ground. "It is the apples you brought to the counter at the market. You left without them. This one goes with the flowers. I wasn't sure there would be a vase in the rental cabin."

"Thank you."

Without being asked, he takes back the bouquet, giving me two hands to open the gift.

Knowing what's inside doesn't diminish my reaction when I remove the tissue wrapped around a textured amber-and-green glass vase with a soft, rolled edge at the top that reminds me of a leaf unfurling. "This is beautiful. I assume it's yours. I'll make sure to return it."

"It's yours. I got it for you."

I turn it over in my hands, tracing the contours and curves. "Is this handblown?"

He nods. "A local artisan."

"It's amazing. I didn't notice anything like this in your store earlier." The truth is, I barely noticed anything other than Ogram from the moment I entered. Still, I'd like to think something as beautiful as this would've at least caught the corner of my eye.

"I don't carry them at Harmony Market. I would of course, happily, but the artist has a shop of their own downtown that keeps them quite busy."

On the surface, Ogram's answer is a simple explanation. With everything I've learned about him, and from Glen's earlier comments, I know the actions he took to get this vase are anything but superficial.

"I love the vase and the flowers." Unintentionally, my voice comes out soft and breathy. Is it because I used the word love? It was about the gift, but the rapid thumping in my chest tells me saying it about him would come just as naturally. A ridiculous thing to think about someone I just met and have spent all of fifteen minutes with. Logically, I know this. Logic doesn't feel like it has a place here, though. "Do you want to come to my cabin while I put them in water?"

He doesn't say anything, just nods, but the way he's looking at me... I can't help wondering if he's feeling the same inexplicable, magnetic pull.

We cross the lawn to my cabin in a matter of seconds. At my door, Ogram doesn't crowd me, giving me an arm's length of space—one of my arms, that is—while I unlock the door with sweaty-palmed hands. He waits until I'm fully inside before following, and that pause gives me the opportunity to turn and watch him enter.

Though the cabins are quaint, freshly painted and very clean, they're not updated. Like the cabinets and fixtures, the doors are from a bygone era, when the standards leaned toward practical rather than grand. Ogram has to duck his head to get through the doorway, and his shoulders barely clear the frame. He's huge. A monster whose species I know nothing about, beyond the little bit he and Glen told me today.

The door clicking closed behind him sounds more like an echo in a cavern than a brief little metallic snick. If I believed the people back home, I'd be terrified right now. Fear is the furthest thing from my mind, and it's sure as heck not the reason my pulse feels like it's doing a lap of the Indianapolis 500.

Ogram's gaze drops to my neck, where I'm sure he can see my pulse hammering. Then lower, to the neckline of my dress. I don't have to look down to know my chest is heaving like a heroine in an old-timey romance novel. All that fictional ready-to-burst anticipation I've devoured over the years makes sense now. I'd like him to lock me in the room, lay me out on the bed, take his cock out and fuck me. Hard, deep, and dominant, as if fucking me is as much about need as it is about want.

The need to come thrums behind my clit, and when I squeeze my thighs together, the slickness there creates an unmistakable sound. A scent too, if Ogram's deep inhalation and flaring nostrils are any indication. But my cheeks don't flame with embarrassment. Not even when his grip on my bouquet tightens as he takes another deep breath.

Unable to help myself, I look at the front of his jeans —and suck in an audible breath. Snug-fitting, they showcase an epic bulge, but not beneath the zipper, where human men tuck their dicks. The thick bulge of Ogram's cock runs down his inner thigh. So far down, it should be alarming, even terrifying, to think of something that size inside me. But I'm not even a teensy bit scared of Ogram's monster.

Forcing my gaze upward, I find his dark eyes waiting. He doesn't speak. Doesn't move—except for thrusting his arm forward to hand off the bouquet. But when I reach for it and our fingers touch, he reacts. A deep rumbling that sounds like hunger, though not the for-food kind.

He retracts his hand and stuffs both into his front pockets. "Perhaps I should wait for you outside."

"Why?"

"I don't wish to make you uncomfortable."

"Having you in my cabin doesn't make me uncomfortable." I let my eyes wander over his hulking form, lingering for a few seconds on the bulge that hasn't gone down, before returning to his face. "Does being in here make *you* uncomfortable?"

The corners of his mouth twitch as if he's fighting back a smile. "I am happy to remain inside with you."

"Good." Smiling, I move toward the sink in the cabin's small kitchenette. When I reach it, I set the vase in the basin and turn the water on low to fill it, then add the flowers, which are already cut to the ideal length for this vase.

Everything about this gift is thoughtful and required personal effort. He may be a monster, but he's already the best man I've ever dated.

"They're perfect together, as if they were made for each other," I say, admiring the vase and blooms while setting the arrangement carefully on the bedside table.

"I think so too." The way he says it pulls my attention to his face, and what I see there makes me think he's not just talking about the vase and flowers.

Heart racing in my chest, I close the distance between us and tip my head back to smile up at him. "I'm ready for our first date."

His thick russet eyebrows rise. "First date?"

"Maybe 'date' is a human term. It's when people spend time together to see if they're a good match romantically. When I asked you out back at your market, I meant as a date. That's what I'd like this evening to be, but if you've decided that's not what you want, don't worry about sparing my feelings, you can just go ahead and tell me. I'll understand if I'm not your type. Oh, and 'your type' means the kind of person you're usually attracted to. Just in case that term isn't familiar either."

For a long beat, he just stares. Processing my incessant, in-your-face straightforwardness, probably. Even for the people back home who claim to care about me, I can be "a lot," and since Ogram is the solitary type, maybe my "a lot" is too much.

"It was the word 'first' that caused me to raise the question," he says, finally. "First implies there will be another."

Groaning, I cup both palms over my face. "And now I feel like an oblivious bumbler—again—assuming you didn't know what 'date' and 'your type' meant. Not to mention assuming you'd want to go out with me a second time."

Despite their large size, his hands are gentle when he draws them away from my face, continuing to hold them in the gap between us. "From what you've told me, you have little experience with the monster community, and prior to meeting me, none with my kind. I wouldn't expect you to be familiar with what trolls know or like or do. Even if you'd spent every minute between our first meeting and now trying to learn about my species, you would still know only the most superficial things. With few exceptions, trolls prefer to remain in the background. We value our privacy, guard it, and have no desire to publicly share the intimate details of our abilities and customs."

The urge to ask him to elaborate on that bit about the intimate details almost wins, but I manage to suppress it. For now.

"I find your openness endearing. Your enthusiasm, delightful and contagious." His eyes twinkle as he looks into mine. "I have never been attracted to a human before, but I was drawn to you the moment you walked into the market, and haven't stopped thinking about you since. To say I hope you will want me to call on you again is an understatement."

"I already know I will, because I felt the same way when I saw you."

His green lips curve into a small but distinct smile. "Then, shall we begin our first date?"

"I think we just did. And it's already the best date I've ever been on."

"Mine as well." Between us, he squeezes my hands. Firmly enough to be inescapably noticeable, gently enough to convey affection.

My feet must be on autopilot because the next thing I know, we're outside, walking down the cabin's small set of concrete steps without any conscious effort on my part. All I can focus on is Ogram's palm at the small of my back. How the warmth of his skin seeps through my sundress and sends sparks skittering through me. How his big hand spans my lower back completely, his fingertips overflowing around the side of my waist.

When I step onto the sidewalk from the bottom step, he removes his hand, and I immediately miss the subtle weight of it.

"You said you're visiting from out of town. How long will you be staying in Harmony Glen?" he asks as we turn onto Glen Street, heading toward downtown and the lake.

"A week and a bit. Minus the three days I've been here." Saying it makes my stomach feel as if it's turning in knots. From the pained expression on Ogram's face, his might be doing the same thing. Over a week here seemed like extended luxury when I made the decision and plans. Now, suddenly, it feels more like I'm on a ticking countdown timer.

"Where do you live?" he asks, breaking through my internal thoughts.

"A town a bit bigger than this in Pennsylvania."

"Pennsylvania isn't far."

"The northern part isn't, but I'm closer to Philadelphia. It took me four and half hours to get here." Not so far away that a long-distance relationship would be impossible, but not close enough to conveniently see each other on a regular basis. Something that shouldn't be crossing my mind on a first date, but it is. It has been since I left Ogram's market store with plans for a date.

Nodding, he pushes his hands into the front pockets of his jeans, when I'd rather he'd reached for my hand to hold. "What do you do there?"

"Waitress. I've worked at the same restaurant forever. Nearly a decade. Just a roadhouse style, but it was a step up from working in fast food because I'd get tips serving tables instead of handing orders across a counter."

"You must be happy there to have stayed on so long."

"More like complacent. The town, the restaurant, the people... they're what I know. It's just easy to keep doing the same thing, even though it's not a good fit anymore."

"Did something happen to change how you feel about your workplace?" Though it's still calm, there's an edge to his voice. Any trace of a smile is gone, and his lips are a thin, tight line that gives his big tusk teeth an almost ferocious prominence.

"Nothing happened to me," I say, slipping my hand through the crook of his arm and curling my fingers over his thick forearm. Beneath my hand, his tense muscles relax. "But every day, the people in my hometown show me their bigoted true selves more than the day before. I'm sure there are people who aren't closed-minded—I can't possibly be the only open-minded one living there—but anytime I speak up in favor of equality for nonhumans, nobody chimes in supportively. Not a peep from anyone. There's plenty of open contempt for integration, though."

"That's unfortunate."

"And that's too kind a word. It's disgusting. I usually stay home during my vacation weeks because traveling isn't something I can afford on my budget, but I took the credit card out of the freezer for this trip. I had to get away for a while." I can't bring myself to tell him the exact reason—what happened to the Wolferd family when they came out as wolf shifters. Even though I was vehemently against it and made my feelings known everywhere possible, I'm still ashamed to be associated with a town that'd treat others that way. "So I got a copy of *Monster Life* magazine—I had to order it, of course, because no stores in town carry it—and chose Harmony Glen from the 'Ten Monster-Inclusive Destinations You Won't Want to Miss This Summer' article."

"I'm glad you did," he says, withdrawing his other hand from his pocket and placing it over mine.

"Me too." Stopped to wait for cars to go by on Lakeview Avenue, I smile up at him. "What about you? Have you always been in Harmony Glen, or did you move here after the Great Revelation?"

The arm I'm holding slides from my grip to wrap protectively around my back as we cross the street. Once we're safely on the sidewalk again, his arm slips away, and he takes my hand, weaving our fingers together with care. "I have always been here, though not openly. I grew up in a small home hidden from human eyes by the way it was built into one of the surrounding hills in a heavily wooded area. The couple who owned the nearby farm and market were aware of my family's existence and always treated us as equals. My parents worked on their land, and when I was old enough, I followed in their footsteps. The owners were ready to retire and offered to sell the property to me the moment integration happened. I will always believe they held on to it as long as possible to ensure I had a job and a safe place."

"I love that." It's the kind of feel-good story that belongs in *Monster Life* magazine, though I doubt he'd want that kind of attention, being solitary as he is.

"It was an extraordinary opportunity for which I was, and am, very grateful."

"Where are they now?"

"The Jensens, the previous owners, are enjoying their golden years in a seniors' condominium apartment overlooking the lake."

"Wow, that's quite a change from living on acres and acres of farmland."

Ogram's big body vibrates with deep chuckling. "I voiced the same thing when they told me their intentions. I offered them to remain in the farmhouse, and I would transform part of the big barn into a bachelor's apartment for myself. They declined, saying they were ready for a different view, and that I would need the house for my family."

Another example of Ogram's kindness. Generosity, too. How humans could see him as anything other than a wonderful person is beyond me. Where I'm from, he'd be vilified, based solely on his exterior. Every minute here, every moment with him, makes me want to never go back. If only that were an option.

"So, your parents live in the farmhouse with you?" I ask, redirecting my thoughts to the present, to learning everything there is to know about my troll. Mine for now, anyway.

He shakes his head, a different kind of smile settling into place. Warm, reverent. "No, they had already passed on by that time. Several years before the Great Revelation. Their spirit lives in the land, though. I feel their presence every time my hands touch the earth."

"That's beautiful," I say, squeezing his hand gently. "I'm sorry for your loss."

"Thank you." Lifting our joined hands, he presses a

soft kiss to my knuckles, the contact bringing butterflies to wing inside me. "I've already mentioned my brother, who no longer resides in this area, so you now know what there is to know about my family. I would like to hear about yours." His eyebrows rise at my grimace. "Unless it's a subject you would rather not discuss."

"No, it's fine. Just...don't hold my shitty parents against me, okay? Because I'm not like them. At all." The fluttering in my chest withers as quickly as it started. "They're anti-integration. Silently at first. Early on, I still believed—or wanted to believe—they'd come around. I tried having calm, logical conversations with them. I thought that eventually *something* I said would click, and they'd realize how narrow-minded and lacking in empathy they'd become."

"Based on your lead-in, I assume that didn't happen."

Shaking my head, I release a defeated sigh. "No, it got worse. As soon as businesses in town started putting up 'Humans Only' signs, normalizing open segregation, my parents jumped on the bandwagon. No more silent hatred, they became part of the bigger, louder, radical problem. They went all-in on hate. Believed the bullshit and lies. That's when I moved into my own place. And when I cut them out of my life."

"That couldn't have been an easy decision."

"I know I should agree, but the sad truth is, they made it easy. Blood made us family. Their toxic beliefs and behavior made us strangers."

Ogram stops, takes my other hand, and holds both while looking into my eyes. "I am sorry for your loss."

I've been so angry at my parents all this time, cutting off contact with them was like a weight being lifted. I never expected or intended to reconnect with them, but the permanence of that hadn't sunk in until this moment, until Ogram's words of condolence. Inside me, on a level deeper than rational thought, deeper than anger and disappointment, something cracks. A single gut-deep sob bubbles out of that fissure before I can suppress it.

In a blink, he pulls me against him, enveloping me in his big arms so completely, it's like being held by a giant teddy bear and an impenetrable force at the same time. An embrace filled with compassion, support, security.

I slide my arms around his waist and press my cheek to his chest. I barely know him, but I know he won't let go until I do. Not because he's polite or feels obligated to comfort me. Because he's good and kind and genuinely cares.

"I've never told anyone about that," I say, resting my chin on his beefy body and looking up at him. "I'm sorry for unloading on you and being a downer on our date."

"Sharing your life stories and feelings with me is a gift I'm honored to receive."

"How is it that somebody as good and kind and sexy as you hasn't been taken off the market yet?" I giggle when his eyebrows shoot up high enough that the top portion disappears beneath his thick, longish auburn hair. "Yes, I said sexy. That's how I feel, and you said sharing my feelings with you is a gift, so consider yourself gifted with the knowledge that I find you incredibly and irresistibly sexy. Oh, and there are no returns or exchanges on this gift."

A blush rises on his cheeks. Again, the muted red with soft edges against his green skin resembles apples, and I can't resist reaching up to brush my fingers over them, accidentally grazing his tusks in the process.

"Sorry—" Before I can pull away, his big hand circles my wrist and guides my fingertips back to the gleaming surface.

"You are always welcome to touch me, Hope. Any part. Anytime."

"If that's your gift to me, there are no returns on it, either."

"No returns," he repeats, his quiet laughter vibrating through me deliciously.

I bite my bottom lip, my heart pounding as if it's trying to break free of my chest, then I slide the pad of my index finger along the long, thick tusk. Despite being permanently outside of his mouth, it's as warm to the touch as an inside tooth would be, and just as smooth. I've never been the run-my tongue-along-your-teeth-while-making-out type, but the urge to do it to Ogram's tusks has my mouth watering.

He still has one arm around me, and it tightens, tugging my lower body tighter to his. The thick bulge of his cock along his thigh presses against me, his nostrils flaring when I scissor my thighs in an attempt to get a hint of friction on my clit. "We should continue on our walk."

"Okay," is what comes out of my mouth, but not

what's really on the tip of my tongue. If he can wait, so can I. Maybe.

OGRAM

The desire roaring inside me is unlike any I have experienced. Not because I have been celibate for the past several years, but because every cell of my being knows without a doubt that Hope is the only person I will sink my cock into for the rest of my days. And if that does not happen, my bed will always be half empty, and my hand will be my cock's only partner. That is the nature of things once a troll meets their mate.

She feels it too. The intense attraction, the undeniable pull, the instant connection.

I won't pressure her to remain in Harmony Glen at the end of her vacation, but I will use every minute she gives me during that time to show her I want her here with me always. Then, perhaps she will stay and make me the happiest monster walking the earth. If that day comes, I will spend the rest of my life making sure she knows the extent of my love and devotion. That I treasure her in every way.

Releasing her from my arms, I once again take her small hand in mine as we resume our walk. Twilight is upon us, bathing our surroundings in a warm glow that wraps around her like a golden hug.

"I didn't tell you how beautiful you are when I arrived at your cabin earlier, and I should have. It was certainly going through my mind."

"Thank you." The beaming smile she gives me is bright enough to make the sun at high noon feel second-rate. "On the subject of not saying things in the moment, you didn't answer my question earlier—how is it possible you're still single? And don't say it's because you don't go out much, because I already know this is a small, tight-knit community, and I'm sure all the singles in town are plenty aware you're a catch." Head turned toward me, her gaze travels down my body, her green eyes twinkling when she meets my eyes again. "A very big catch."

Again, amusement rumbles through me. "I've lost track of how many times I've smiled and laughed this evening. More than I have in a long stretch. I know that's due to my tendency to avoid social settings, limiting my opportunities to enjoy humor with others, but I never felt like it was something missing from my life."

"You're enjoying it tonight, though? The smiling and laughing?"

"Very much." So much, in fact, that I've barely regis-tered the people we've passed, even when I felt the weight of their stares.

"I'm glad," she says, squeezing my hand. "But don't think I haven't noticed that you're still avoiding my question. If it was too personal, you can tell me. *Should* tell me. Otherwise, you can count on me coming back to it because I'm invested in the answer."

And I am invested in her reaction to it. "The beach looks quite private this evening," I say as we reach a narrow, convenient spot to cross to the shoreline. "How do you feel about sand between your toes while I answer?"

"I would love that." She briefly tilts her head downward. "Though I might not want to put these shoes back on afterward."

"I'm sure I can find something to clean and dry your feet with."

"Ooh, tempting as *that* sounds, it's not what I meant. I might not want to put them back on again because they're like implements of torture." Her free, easy laughter carries across the evening air.

"If the shoes hurt your feet so badly, why did you wear them?"

"Because that's what human women do when they want to impress their date. We wear heels that kill our feet, dresses that don't leave room to breathe, underwire bras that dig in and leave marks but make our boobs look good, and skimpy underwear that serves no purpose other than tempting our date to remove them."

My mind swims with thoughts of what she's wearing under her dress. Thoughts that make my cock thicken and press against the seam of my pants. This is not the time or place to share those reactions with her. "You don't need any of those things to impress me."

"You're sweet."

"Not entirely," I say, enjoying the way her eyes pop wide open, along with her mouth. "Since we're speaking honestly."

"You know you're going to have to elaborate on that missile, right?"

"Missile?"

"Missile, as in, you dropped a bomb and hit the target. Your missile was a deliberately vague comment you knew would surprise and entice me."

"True. That was my hope."

"And that kind of straightforward honesty is another reason you're a catch."

"Then you are also a catch."

She snorts a laugh. "That's not how it works. I've never met a man who considered straightforward honesty in a woman as an 'ooh, she's a catch' quality." Steadying herself against me, she reaches down and removes her shoes, sighing with relief once she's free of them. "I can't believe I made it this far in these heels. I'll say goodbye to them tomorrow at that thrift shop I saw downtown. Nifty Thrifty. Cute name for a cute shop in a cute town. Everything here is idyllic."

"It's a good place to live. If you ask around, I don't think you'll find a single person who regrets moving here."

"Sounds like the farmer is planting seeds," she says, smiling up at me. Always smiling. Always genuine.

"Perhaps I am." I wait until she's taken my hand again and we've started across the sand to circle back to her earlier comment. "These other men you've met who don't value straightforwardness as highly as they should, did you want any of them to catch you?"

"Definitely not. I never liked anyone enough to even consider having a commitment, especially something long-term. And since they didn't reach out to see me again either, they obviously felt as underwhelmed by our dates as I did."

A solid answer, but lacking some specifics I hoped to learn. "And if you were to meet someone who didn't disappoint you, would you wish to be caught then?"

At the water's edge, she stops rather than follow the shoreline. "I might," she says, releasing my hand and turning to face me. "I didn't grow up with commitment on my mind, but I'm not against it, either. With the right person. This will probably sound unrealistic, and maybe old-fashioned, but if I'd only make it official and get married if I was sure in my heart and gut and soul that the relationship would stand the test of time. Which is ridiculous, of course, because it's impossible to know that. There are never guarantees."

I swallow down the urge to tell her there *are* guarantees. That the bond between mates doesn't just endure, it grows and blooms, flourishing from the connection. That I am that person for her, as she is for me. Too soon, even though I know she feels our connection is something more than casual attraction. More than the result of a chance encounter.

With the lake at her back and the sun hovering just above the horizon, she almost glows. An aura that seems to grow brighter with her smile when she playfully pokes my chest. "Your turn. No wiggling out of it with distractions this time. And after you're done telling me why you're still on the market, you can give me the details as to how you're 'not entirely' sweet. And don't worry about shocking me—I'm a diehard spicy romance reader."

In all the years I've longed to meet my mate, I never imagined fate would choose a human. Nor someone outgoing and outspoken, regardless of their species. Now that I've met her, it makes sense. She is what my life was missing. I can only hope she will feel the same about me, because the thought of her leaving Harmony Glen makes my insides tighten into knots.

She gasps as the lake sends a wave far enough onto the beach to cover the tops of her feet. "I didn't realize I was close enough to get wet," she says, looking over her shoulder at the retreating water. "It's nice, though. Warmer than I expected for early autumn. I think I'll wade through it while we walk."

"I'll join you."

Her gaze follows me as I crouch. Stays on me while I remove my shoes and stuff the socks into the toes, then roll up my jeans until they're just below my knees. When I straighten and step deeper into the water, offering my hand, she smiles wide, her lovely teeth gleaming, like the full moon in a cloudless sky.

"This is perfect," she says loudly enough to hear over

the rhythmic splashing we're creating with each step. "I guess trolls like water?"

"Trolls are deeply connected with nature, and though most of our affinity is with the earth and plants, we enjoy the water as well."

"In that case, would you like to go swimming with me sometime? There's no swimmable natural water of any kind in my hometown, so I'd love to go out in the lake while I'm here, even though it's kind of late in the season. I could go by myself during the daytime, but I'd rather go with you. Only if you want to, of course. If you do, we could come back another evening, so there are fewer people you'd have to be around."

The *while I'm here* is like a punch to my gut and soul, but the hope I get from her willingness to accommodate my preference for solitude so we can spend time together is a counterbalance to the negative sensation. "I would like that very much. An evening swim here would be a good way for you to experience the freedom of open-water lake swimming. And if you want to try something different another day, I could take you to a place where I swim whenever I have time."

"Ooh, I'm totally down. And intrigued. Is it in the river somewhere, or one of the little creek offshoots?"

Though an explanation is unnecessary, I wait a moment to see if she'll tell me what *totally down* means, as she has with other terms. This time, she doesn't. A sign that we're getting to know each other, I think.

"Nothing like that. There's a swimming hole in the woods beyond my farm's fields, near the home where I grew up. It's not large, just a few strokes to get from one side to the other, but the small size and shallow depth make the water temperature warmer than the lake, especially now that summer is over. That area is very private, though, and if the idea of being somewhere secluded makes you uneasy—"

"It doesn't. Not if you're there with me. That probably makes me sound ridiculously naïve. No sensible woman would put full trust in a man she just met, especially when he's twice her size and has the advantage of knowing the lay of the land. And I'm not usually like this. Actually, I'm *never* like this. Especially in past five years, since I've discovered that so many people are shitty at their core. But there's something, something I can't logically explain, that makes me sure I'm safe with you."

This is the perfect opportunity to tell her about our bond. That we're meant to be together. But I'd rather she discover that herself. "You can trust your feelings. I would never harm you in any way, nor allow anyone else to do so in my presence."

"See, there you go, being sweet again, even though you *claim* you're not entirely sweet." Even in the dimming light, the twinkle in her eyes is unmistakable. "And that's a subtle reminder—or not-so-subtle since I'm pointing it out—that I'm still waiting for your answers."

Again, amusement rumbles within me. "Which would you like first? The reason I had no romantic attachments when you walked into my market store, or how I'm not entirely sweet?"

"Start with why you're single. I have a feeling the other information is going to short-circuit my brain."

If that's all it does, I'll count myself lucky. She might end our first date and decline to have another. But if we are to have more of these moments, if the chemistry between us leads to physical intimacy, she needs to know what that entails.

First, to explain my unattached status. "Trolls don't have a need for social connection, and that includes dating for casual companionship, or for the purpose of selecting a mate."

"What about for sex?" she asks before I can continue.

"We do, on occasion, engage in sexually gratifying activities with others. Perhaps less commonly than many species, though."

"Because your solitary lifestyle means you encounter fewer people to possibly have sex with, I assume."

"That is part of it. The other part will address the second answer you're waiting for." Knowing I'm about to discuss the intimate details of troll mating with her causes my cock to thicken, its solidity pressing into my thigh and its denim enclosure. "Male trolls are...large. Not an issue when coupling with female trolls, but other species some-times find it...too much."

Her bottom lip drops, her eyes opening wide, as if they might pop out of her face. "As in, it literally doesn't fit?"

"To the best of my knowledge, male trolls will only experience arousal if intercourse is possible, though it may require preparation with smaller species."

"Preparation," she says slowly, as if each syllable of the word is a puzzle piece and she's fitting them together. Then she gasps.

Her intimate perfume fills my nose, my head, and I can't resist drawing a deep breath, pulling it into the back of my throat so I can almost taste her.

"There is more."

"Tell me." Her breathy tone is one I long to hear while pleasuring her.

"When coupling, especially while a female is in the fertile portion of her cycle, male trolls often enter a rut, making it nearly impossible to stop once coitus has begun. Females of another species may find it...intense."

She just stares up at me, holding my gaze as we continue wading through water neither of us spares a glance.

"Perhaps I shouldn't have shared those details on our first date."

"But you did. Consciously or subconsciously, you must have wanted to tell me about troll sex, or you wouldn't have made that earlier comment about not being entirely sweet that you knew would pique my curiosity. My guess is that you wanted to see how I'd react, if I'd be shocked, scared, and disgusted, or the opposite." Her fingers squeeze mine, and she smiles. "Count me in for the opposite. But I do have questions."

"I will answer without delay this time."

"You know, I'm enjoying everything about our date, including the delays."

"So am I." I leave it at that, even though I'm tempted

to steer the conversation in another direction, solely so she may tease me about doing so.

"Honest answers only, okay?" Just for a moment, her confident expression wavers, so quickly I might have missed it if not entirely engrossed in her every gesture.

"You have my word."

Nodding, she takes a breath and pulls her bottom lip between her teeth, then releases both, along with a flurried, "Is this a sex date?"

"No," I blurt, louder than normal or necessary.

She slants her head while making a throaty, close-mouthed *hmm*. "You look mortified that I asked."

"Because I am."

"Don't be. I'm not offended or anything like that. I'm a modern, twenty-eight-year-old woman, and if I want to have casual sex with someone, I can and will, because sex isn't wrong or dirty or off-limits. That said, I'm *not* someone who frequently jumps into bed with people. But I am very attracted to you. So, if sex *is* why you said yes to coming out with me tonight—"

"It isn't," I say, stopping and facing her. "Though I won't deny desiring you more than anyone I've ever met."

"Well, that's flattering, except that I know you don't meet a lot of people."

A chuckle slips out before I can stifle it.

Fortunately, she doesn't seem upset by my reaction. A smile accompanies a little shake of her head that makes her dark hair glimmer in the burgeoning moonlight. "You weren't looking to get sex tonight, you prefer not socialize in general, and trolls don't date for casual companionship or to weed out candidates while searching for a mate. So, why *are* you here with me?"

"Because I was drawn to you the moment I saw you. A sexual attraction, certainly, but more than that. You're the first—the only—person I've wanted to spend time with, rather than be alone. A sensation I haven't experienced before. Something I'd begun to think I might never feel."

"That's a pretty perfect answer."

"It's the truth." Not the entire truth, but telling her on our first date that I know in the depths of my heart and soul she is the one for me would be too much. For a human, anyway. If she were a troll, there would be no need for dates or explanations. She would know as clearly as I do. But our path is unique. And so far, I am enjoying this path with her very much.

"I have one more question," she says, smiling up at me so fully, so openly, I feel it as much as I see it. "Humans kiss for a bunch of different reasons, including romance and sexual passion. Is kissing part of troll intimacy?"

There are two possible ways to answer. A safe, polite, verbal yes. Or what I do.

Chapter Five

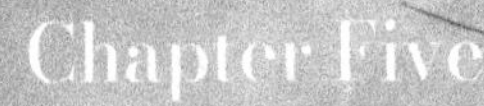

HOPE

"I have one more question." At this exact moment, that is. The more I learn about him, the more I want to know. Right now, though, I really want the answer to *this* question, because those tusk teeth of his are going to make kissing very interesting—if his answer is yes. "Humans kiss for a bunch of different reasons, including romance and sexual passion. Is kissing part of troll intimacy?"

Sunset's glow reflects off the water, making his dark eyes twinkle. For a beat, he's silent, and I'm sure he's deciding how to carefully word his answer. Then, his big hand is beneath my chin, tipping it up while leaning in and bringing his mouth to mine. His lips are soft, the kiss gentle yet firm as he teases the seam of my lips with his tongue.

I open for him, our breath mingling and tongues meeting. Sparks rocket through me, and I shamelessly moan into his mouth. He responds with a deep rumble, his hand sliding around my neck to the back of my head. His fingers tangle in my hair while he adjusts the angle of our kiss, causing one of his tusk teeth to press against my cheek.

So. Hot. It takes conscious effort to hang on to my

shoes instead of dropping them into the lake and wrapping my arms around him so I can climb him like a tree. Instead, I use my free hand to unbutton his shirt to where it's tucked into his jeans, then press my palm against his bare chest.

Another rumble vibrates through our kiss, then he pulls back, leaving me breathless and blinking up at him.

"Don't stop," I whisper, my body tingling and ready for more. So much more. But with each passing second of silent staring instead of tangling tongues, the fire he ignited inside me sputters. "I thought you liked it as much as I did."

"Perhaps more."

I cough a little laugh. "Um, I don't think that's possible. I was about five seconds away from asking you to take me home and do whatever *preparation* you need to do so this could become a sex date."

On a long exhale, his fingers leave the back of my head, sifting through the length of my hair before settling over my hand where it still sits on his chest. "I want you in my bed, make no mistake of that. But not simply for a night of sexual gratification. That's not how I see you."

There's that sweetness again. "We could have multiple nights. All the nights I'm here, or as many of them as you want, anyway. Hooking up wasn't on my vacation itinerary, and..."

"You said 'and' not 'but,'" he says when I don't complete my thought. "And what?"

"And I know how ridiculous this is going to sound on a first date, after one kiss. *And* I know the logistics of what I'm about to say are not great because you're a farmer with more daily responsibility than I can imagine, *and* I live four and a half hours away. *And* I know I'm assuming a lot by saying any of this. But—see, there is a 'but'—" I wink up at him, and his chest vibrates with a silent chuckle. "I don't see you as a vacation hookup. I would accept this being a temporary thing if that's what you wanted—"

"It isn't."

Seconds slide by with only the sounds of nature filling the air. The gentle, rhythmic lapping of waves. Faint birdsong, probably from the trees, which are now dark silhouettes beyond the shoreline.

I fight the urge to say more. Ask more. Talk until everything is hammered out and pinned down to within an inch of its life. To talk for the sake of talking. But Ogram seems perfectly at ease with the pause. The calm quiet. And of course, he does—he's told me multiple times that he's a solitary creature. If this date has any hope of becoming more than a one-off, more than a vacation fling, I need to get comfortable with Ogram's preference for...less.

"Okay." That's all I allow myself to say. Holding my tongue and keeping my lips closed, I smile intentionally, the way I would if I were having a posed photo taken. Against my will.

Based on how high his eyebrows rise, my expression must look as unnatural as it feels.

Seven seconds. That's how long I hold my *me*-ness in

before releasing a pained sigh of defeat. "I don't know if I can do it."

"Do what?" he asks, his eyebrows descending lower than their usual resting place.

"Resist talking. Babbling. Silence isn't my natural state, as I'm sure you're already aware. But you've stepped out of your lane tonight, and I really want to make an effort to meet you in yours."

The final word is barely out of my mouth when he wraps one arm around my waist, pulls me tight against him, and kisses me. This time, I don't need him to adjust our angles, I just melt beneath him, tilting and opening and getting lost in the taste and feel of him.

"Feel free to shut me up that way anytime," I say when he breaks the kiss, presumably so we don't pass out from lack of breathing.

The joke falls flat, his eyebrows pulling together at the bridge of his nose as he releases me and takes a step backward. "That is not why I kissed you."

"I was just teasing," I say, but it's not enough to change the way he's looking at me.

Maybe because he knows it's not entirely true.

A dog barks as it runs up the beach, the sharp sound bursting the metaphorical bubble around us.

"Sorry to interrupt!" the dog's owner calls, waving at us as he trails behind his bounding canine. "Have a great night!"

Automatically and without speaking, we return the polite gesture, our arms dropping once the man's back is to us.

"I would never do something to silence you," Ogram says before I can get a word out. "I kissed you because I wanted to. In that moment, I wanted to because, even though we are just beginning, you once again considered my needs and preferences, and you were willing to put them above your own comfort."

"An unsuccessful attempt that lasted less than ten seconds, but of course I tried. I'll continue to try."

"I don't want you to do that," he says, taking my free hand in his. "I enjoy everything about you, just as you are, and I would not change a single thing."

Swoon. Seriously. "Okay, but if I ever just talk too damn much and you've had enough for a while, please tell me, okay?"

"I will agree, though only to give you peace of mind."

Shaking my head, I snort a laugh. "You'll get sick of my nonstop talking. Everyone does."

"I am not everyone."

It's true. Not because he's green and huge, or any of the other superficial qualities that make him different. Because he's good, kind, thoughtful, sweet, gentlemanly, *and* sexy, all at the same time. "I know you're not."

"Good." He squeezes my hand gently. "Never curb your expressiveness with me. Your voice is beautiful. Like music to my ears," he says, angling his head to provide a better view of the tall, pointed green flesh in question. "And trolls' ears are quite sensitive."

"Hearing-wise, you mean. Or, as in, sensitive to the touch?"

"Both."

And now I want to reach up and touch them to see just how sensitive they really are. But if ear play is the thing that'll unravel him, I'd rather not be ankle-deep in a lake when I find out.

Stepping to my side, he tucks my hand through the crook of his elbow, carefully folding my fingers over his massive forearm. "Shall we make our way over to the boardwalk and head back to your cabin?" He tilts his head at the unspoken question that must be written on my face. "Where I will say goodnight to you at the door."

"You could come in instead. It wouldn't be a sex date. It'd be a date that includes sex." I huff when his big body rumbles with amusement. The irritation doesn't last—it's just a little sexual frustration. More than a little, actually, and that's new for me. Sex has always been a take-it-or-leave-it thing. After kissing Ogram, I want to take it all and take it now. "Waiting for another time is important to you?"

"It is."

"Then it's important to me too," I say as we resume walking.

Water gives way to wet sand that squishes up between my toes with each step, then dry sand that sticks to my skin everywhere the water touched. We reach the boardwalk and I rub my feet against the smooth wooden slats. Then each foot against the opposite leg. Some of the sand falls away, but not enough to be rid of the crusty, prickly layer so uncomfortable and distracting, it threatens to suck all the good feelings out of my mind.

"Allow me to help," Ogram says, crouching before me and placing one of my feet on his knee.

The sun has set and the moon hangs in its place, joining with the streetlamps dotting the boardwalk to bathe the area is subtle white light. Enough light for me to see the muscles flexing and moving beneath the shirt stretched taut across his shoulders and back, and how small my foot looks between his large green hands as he gently brushes the sand from my skin.

Having sand removed from my feet should not be an erotic experience. Tell that to every nerve ending in my body. Each swipe of his palm is like a tug on an invisible thread anchored between my legs. By the time he moves to my second foot, I'm biting my bottom lip to hold back a moan that belongs behind a closed bedroom door, not on the beach boardwalk. My knees go into jelly mode, and I sway a bit.

"I have you," he says, his hand molding to the dip of my waist. "Hold my shoulders if you need to."

Need? Oh, I need. Just not in the way he means. Placing my hands on his shoulders does the opposite of steadying me. My palms seem to have a mind of their own, sweeping over every broad, solid inch I can reach before moving to his ears, where I trace one long, erect point with the tip of my index finger. "Should I stop?" I ask when he tenses beneath my touch.

"It is best if you do." Returning my foot to the ground, he grips my hips with both hands and holds me firmly while leaning in and pressing his face against my dress, his nose nudging the fabric between my thighs. He inhales deeply, then looks up at me with hungry eyes. "I want you more than you can imagine, Hope."

"I want you too, so why are we fighting it?"

"Because, the way your scent is affecting me, I'm not certain I could resist rutting were I to be inside you."

"What if I don't want you to resist?" For a split second, there's wildness in his eyes, and I think—no, I hope—he's about to fold me over his shoulder and cart me off to some shadowy spot and make good on his words.

Then he rises, nostrils flaring and chest heaving as if he's just exerted himself. "There is more to the rut than deep, relentless penetration."

"Just so you know, saying you'll give me 'deep, relentless penetration' is doing the opposite of scaring me off." It's part teasing, part flirting, and based on his unflinching intensity, neither thing hits the mark. "Okay, I'm listening. Tell me the 'more' that you think I won't be able to handle."

"The rut is nature's way of assuring species continuation."

"Species continuation?" *Oh.* My mouth goes dry and my panties do the opposite. "As in, you'd be intentionally trying to...impregnate me?"

"Yes." That single word comes out deeper than any other he's said to me.

I've never given motherhood or children much consideration, and what little thought I *have* mustered on the subject sure didn't happen on a first date. But none of those dates were with Ogram.

Wildly premature as it is, I can picture myself with a

big round belly and Ogram by my side. Imagining a family with him is like one of those blissful, soft-around-the-edges dreams that happen in the place between awake and asleep. The kind you never want to end.

"Now you understand why I must be careful." His calm, even-toned voice snaps me out of the fairy-tale vision.

"Because you don't want to get me pregnant."

"No," he says, shaking his head. "Because I do."

Chapter Six

OGRAM

After a long day, I drive the tractor into the drop-off area outside the barn, pulling a wagon carrying full bins from this afternoon's apple harvesting. My farmworkers are deservedly on their way home, and I intend to fill my remaining waking hours with jobs I can do alone. Much like any other day, aside from my mind not being focused on the tasks at hand.

All I can think about is Hope. Her spirit and honesty and humor. Her beautiful smile and voice and laughter. The silkiness of her hair and softness of her skin. How sweet her lips and breath tasted when we kissed. How desperately I wanted to taste the rest of her before sinking my cock into her well-satisfied, willing body, where I'd rut until my cum didn't just fill her, it over-flowed from her thoroughly fucked cunt. Then I'd do it all over again.

Now I never will. Any chance I had of claiming my mate is gone. I knew it the moment I admitted the entirety of my desires. Too much troll truth, far too soon. The shock on her face when she looked at me was only surpassed by her quietness during the walk to her cabin. Silence in opposition to her natural tendency for conversation. I didn't kiss her goodnight or ask for another date. Nor did she.

Finding my mate, the most important event of my life, and I ruined it on our first date.

I climb down from the tractor, shaking my head as I walk toward the drive shed to get the forklift. Halfway there, I freeze on the spot, tilting my head back to catch a scent on the evening breeze. Her scent.

"Hi." She gives a little wave as I turn in her direction. Today she's wearing jeans and a floral shirt that's tied in a knot at her waist, and white sneakers that have no place on a farm. Much like their wearer, even though I want nothing more than to see her here every day until forever runs out.

"I didn't expect to see you today." Or ever again, though I keep those words to myself. I would rather have her disgust than her pity.

"I was here earlier. Well, not *here*, here. In the Harmony Market store. I thought you'd be there on a Saturday, but your employees told me you were working in the field all day."

"Farming doesn't care about weekends, especially in harvest season. We wait months for crops to be ready, then have a brief window to reap everything before poor weather and cool temperatures arrive."

"And right now, it's apple season."

"Other things too, but apples are among the more sought-after crops we farm here."

"You say 'we' often when you're talking about the farm. I thought you were the sole owner."

"Owner is just a name on a deed. Everyone who works here is an equally important part of the farm."

"I love that," she says, moving toward me until she's so close, she has to tip her head back to smile up at me. "You have a green leaf in your hair. A little branch piece too."

"Probably more than one of each and maybe some bugs." I can't help chuckling when her eyes open wide and she takes a step back. City folks. "We pick apples by hand. Have to get right in the trees."

"That sounds fun. Except for the bugs in the hair part. And the having to do it all day part."

"We have a pick-your-own area if you want to give it a try while you're in town. Stop into the market store and they'll get you sorted, tell you where to go and how to pick."

"Or...maybe you could show me? I'd say 'sometime when you're not busy,' but—"

"Tell me when you'd like to do it and I'll make time." The words leave my lips before my brain has a chance to catch up. If I sound desperate, it's because I am. I don't expect another chance to have her as my mate, but I'll take any kind of moment with her I can get.

"It could be our next date." When I fail to respond with words, she fidgets with the knot at her waist and the lock of hair already tucked tidily in place behind one ear. "Unless that's too much like work for you to have a good time."

"I would sit and stare at dirt with you if that's what you wanted, and enjoy every second. Any time spent with you is much better than good."

Her relief is almost tangible when she blows out a breath. "Oh, thank goodness. I thought you might not feel that way after I barely spoke to you during the walk back to my cabin last night, and the way we left things."

"It is I who caused the tone of our evening to shift, not you."

"I think we both did. The information you shared was a lot to digest, no question. And that's what I had to do—digest it. Repeatedly, like a cow, until I'd thoroughly processed it all."

"Were you able to do that?"

"Yes." She nods. "I think so."

I have no right to feel optimistic, but the feeling rises regardless. Not enough to question her further, though. Whatever she might say must be on her timeline.

"You said the rut often happens when a female partner is fertile, and you told me—" Color floods her cheeks, painting them like summer roses. "You told me that my scent was affecting you enough to send you into a rut if we had sex. So, does that mean you can *smell* me ovulating? Because I checked my calendar when I was back at the cabin last night, and it was day thirteen of my cycle, which the internet seems to agree is go time if you're trying to get pregnant."

There is no willing my cock to remain flaccid. Tucked inside my pant leg, it grows thick and hard and ready for her, precum rolling down my inner thigh. "Yes, your scent holds distinct markers, including your body's fertility."

"No wonder you don't care to be out among groups of people. Being bombarded by the smell of fertile females must be overwhelming and um," her gaze lowers to the obvious bulge of my hard cock, "uncomfortable."

Shaking my head sends the debris from the apple trees floating to the ground. "That is not how it is. Though our sense of smell is more heightened than a human's, male trolls aren't attuned to the markers of every female's scent."

"Only the ones you're attracted to?"

"Yes." The simplest answer, and the safest. "I apologize for scaring you. I was far too forthcoming last night. I realize you don't know me well enough to be assured by words, but I promise you that I would never act on my desires without consent."

"I believe you. I trust you. And I wasn't scared. Not in the way you mean," she says, stepping closer again. "I don't understand it, honestly. If any other man said even a fraction of the things you did, I would've ended the date on the spot. But from you, with you, I wasn't turned off, I was turned *on*. I didn't want to run home and lock the door and maybe get a restraining order. I wanted you to rut with me. On me? Whichever. I wanted everything you told me would happen. *That's* what scared me. I just met you, yet I wanted you to indulge your primal instincts and...breed me." The last two words come out quieter than the others. Breathier.

Rosy pink flushes her skin and the scent of her arousal perfumes the air. Even without inhaling deeply, I can almost taste her on the back of my tongue.

"Those feelings, they shocked me," she says. "I needed time to think without my hormones distracting me. Giving in to the heat of the moment would've been incredible, but after that moment, the consequences..."

Becoming pregnant with our child. Becoming my mate. She considers those things consequences.

"I can barely support *myself* on my income, and that's if I'll even have a job waiting when I go back, because I didn't leave on the best of terms with my boss. Or my community."

Stunned that she thinks I would put the responsibility and gift of raising our child entirely on her, I just stare. Wait, because I can tell she has more to say, and that she's unaware of the affront to my honor.

"I'm not ready for that, so I stopped at one of the stores and bought some contraceptives. Not condoms, obviously, after what you said about being, um," again, her gaze drops to the prominent bulge of my cock, "large." Her cheeks deepen to red when she meets my eyes. "So I bought sponges."

"Cleaning products are used to prevent pregnancy in humans?"

She sputters and snorts, her lips curving into a glorious, full smile. "Not cleaning sponges. Vaginal sponges. One is inserted before sex."

"I am not familiar with this item, but if it was designed to absorb human semen, one will be inadequate with me. You would need to insert many sponges if you hope to absorb the full volume of my ejaculate."

By the time I finish speaking, tears are running down her cheeks and her body is shaking with amusement. "It doesn't work by absorbing all the cum," she says, gripping my arm for support as she bends at the waist, giggling uncontrollably.

"But that's what sponges do—absorb liquid."

"Oh, my stomach," she groans, folding her other arm across her middle. She gasps when I scoop her off her feet, wrapping her arms behind my neck as I carry her into the drive shed, where I set her carefully on a large storage box.

Crouching in front of her, I gently smooth her hair from her face. "Do you need medical assistance?"

She catches my hand and presses her cheek against my palm, smiling at me. "It's just a stitch from laughing. You're so sweet." Turning her face, she presses a kiss to my work-roughened skin before breathing me in. "You even smell sweet."

"From the apples. I haven't washed up yet."

Her gaze travels to the top of my head, then she releases my hand so she can carefully extract another remnant from working in the orchard. Dropping the leaf to the ground, she threads her fingers through my hair, first one hand, then both. Her gentle, deliberate touch renders me powerless.

Unable to resist, I groan at the like rake of her nails against my scalp. Close my eyes when she switches to a massaging motion with her fingertips.

"Ogram," she says quietly. She's biting her lip when I open my eyes. "Can I tell you something? Something serious."

"Telling me about inserting sponges in your vagina wasn't serious?"

Another infectious giggle leaves her smiling lips. "I suppose it was."

"You never have to ask. Anything you wish to say to me, I want to hear it."

"That's going to take some getting used to. Most people tune me out, or come right out and tell me to stop talking, but you actually want to listen." Her hands leave my hair and fall to her sides, her shoulders drooping, even as she gives me a half smile. "People assume that because I'm a nonstop talker, I must be shallow. Like I don't have the capacity for depth because I'm a motormouth. But that's not true."

Hearing that others have judged her, hurt her, awakens feelings I have never before experienced. More than protectiveness. A willingness, readiness, to avenge. It swirls like a tornado inside me, its power spreading through me until I feel the tingle in my fingertips. A sensation not unlike the green magic trolls possess because of our connection to the earth, but lacking clarity of purpose.

"I do not think you're shallow," I say, curling my fingers toward my palms.

"I'm glad." She reaches for one of my fists, molding her delicate fingers over the back of my hand. If she feels the energy I'm trying to suppress, it doesn't register as such, though her face does brighten as our skin meets. "I came to Harmony Glen to experience a monster-integrated community, but I had no intention of getting involved with anyone, of any species, or having sex on this trip. Then you happened. I just want you to know that wanting to have sex with you isn't just about sex. It's about you."

Our bond as mates, she feels it. Acknowledges it in her own way.

"This is where you say something so I know if you believe me or—"

"There is no 'or,'" I say, cupping the back of her head in my palm and bringing my mouth to hers.

Her soft gasp quickly becomes a moan, her fingers once again threading through my hair as she opens for me, both lips and legs.

I take both invitations, dropping to my knees between her thighs, pressing against her everywhere possible and kissing her deeply enough to taste her soul. Her beautiful, warm, open soul.

She wraps her legs around me, pulling me tighter. "I want you," she whispers on a breath between hungry kisses.

"And I, you, but it will require preparation."

"Then prepare me. Please," she says, guiding my hand to the front of her jeans.

I pop the button and lower the zipper, licking my lips as I slide my fingers down the exposed V of soft skin, then beneath the edge of thin pink lace. "Gods, I want to devour you," I murmur against her neck as my finger slides through the soft warm slickness of her crease.

"Oh, whoa, sorry," are the words I hear next. Not from my mate. "Didn't think anyone was here."

Withdrawing my hand, I refasten Hope's pants before standing in front of her to block her from my employee's view. "I thought everyone had gone for the day."

"Yeah, we did. I got halfway home, then remembered Maryanne telling me to bring a bushel of apples so she can make two hundred turnovers for the elementary school bake sale, so I circled back. Saw the trailer sitting unloaded when I came around and figured you must've been called away before you got the bins off the wagon, so I thought I'd grab the forklift and take care of them before the storm rolls in." Andy hooks a thumb toward the sky outside. "Rain's on the way in. Maybe five minutes out, max."

Good man, good intentions, bad timing. "I appreciate you stepping up. Just got sidetracked talking, but I'll get the apples unloaded and stacked now. Grab whatever you need and give your wife my best."

"Will do," he says, nodding. "Have a good night."

Once he's out of view, I step to the drive shed's opening and listen for the sound of his engine in the parking lot, then for gravel crunching under tires. Satisfied we're truly alone, I turn and find Hope standing nearby.

"Sorry for putting you in an awkward situation with one of your employees," she says.

"You have nothing to apologize for. *I* am sorry for compromising you. I should not have touched you without the guarantee of privacy."

"I think it's safe to say neither of us was aware the rest of the world even existed in that moment." Eyes twinkling and lips curved in a smile, she points toward the sky. "But I think your guy is right about the rain. Is there any way I can help? I know literally nothing about farming or equipment, but I take direction well and I'm not afraid to work my butt off."

Her offer brings my heart joy. But she's not dressed for farm work, explaining even the basic tasks would take time to ensure she's safe on the job, and raindrops have begun to dot the ground, with the clouds appearing ready to erupt.

"Don't worry about gently declining my help, Ogram. I know I'd just slow you down. Go do what you need to do. I'll wait."

"I have two more wagons to bring in from the field after these bins are unloaded and stacked, then some other jobs to do before I can dedicate my attention to you the way you deserve."

"Even your dirty talk is sweet," she says, stepping close enough to pull me down for a kiss. "And that was the nicest 'get out of here' I've ever heard." Giggling at the obvious distress on my face—because I absolutely did not instruct her to get out of here—she kisses me again, then moves away, waving as she walks backward in the direction of the parking lot. "I'm going to The Corner Bar to listen to a vampire opera singer perform! Can you believe that? I love it here! I left my number with the girl in the market store today, so text me whenever you're ready to dedicate your attention to me the way I deserve, and I'll hurry back to do the same—or test the limits of my gag reflex trying, anyway!"

Tempting as her suggestion is, I have another plan. One she won't expect. Something I never expected to do, especially voluntarily. But for her, with her, I'd do just about anything.

Chapter Seven

HOPE

The Corner Bar is as cozy and charming inside as its red-brick exterior. Despite being early autumn and past the summer tourist season, the pub is shoulder to shoulder with patrons, and has been since shortly after I arrived.

After not being able to catch a server's attention through Mari, the hauntingly beautiful vampire *former* opera singer's, first set, I lined up at the bar. Nobody seemed to notice or care about the wide variety of species with whom they were sharing closed quarters. Another example of how different Harmony Glen is from my hometown.

When I finally reached the polished wood with its classic bronze rail, a forty-something blonde woman with a fading summer tan, warm hazel eyes, and natural beauty welcomed me with a kind but unmistakably tired smile. Whether it's food or drinks, the job is essentially the same, and I know the look of someone who's doing more than one person's work.

That's why instead of ordering a drink, I offered to stand in for whoever no-showed or called in sick. And to my happy surprise, the woman—Cate, the bar owner—accepted.

Which is why I'm weaving through the crowd with a tray of drinks perched on one ever-steady hand when I spot him. *Him*, him. Waving my free hand, I catch his eye and give him what I hope is the universal signal to wait right there. Then serve out the orders at lightning speed.

"You're here," I squeal when I reach him. "Oh shit, did I miss your message, and you're here because I didn't answer?" I fish my phone out of my pocket, but he catches my hand before I can swipe the screen to check notifications.

"I'm here to join you, if the invitation from yesterday still stands."

The invitation. My *duh* moment when I asked him to go to bar with me immediately after he told me he doesn't do well in group settings. An invitation he declined, albeit it indirectly. And now he's here. Someone who prefers solitude, in what must be the most crowded place in town this Saturday night. To be with me.

"If that is no longer what you want..." he says when I continue to silently gape.

"I do, it is, it definitely is, I'm just shocked speechless, is all. Which is shocking in itself, I know. But it's good silent. Happy silent. Really happy." Then I remember there's a serving tray hanging from my other hand.

"Shoot, but I'm also working, and I don't want to let Cate down. She's the owner, but you probably knew that since you've both been in the area for years, and I know you have a lot of business connections through the farm. She was so relieved when I offered to cover because she was short-staffed tonight."

Ogram's thick eyebrows pinch together at the bridge of his nose. "You know Cate?"

"I do now. I met her tonight."

"You came to listen to a singing performance, and now you work here." It's a statement, but he says it slowly, as if he's trying to make sense of it.

"Well, I'm working here *tonight*, but," I let my gaze drift around the busy pub, "I'd say yes if Cate asked me to help out again."

"While you're on vacation?"

The question snaps my attention back to Ogram. It's a simple question. Yes or no. My answer definitely isn't no, but yes isn't right, either. So I hum "mm-hmm" and nod.

And get a single nod in return. "I understand."

But he doesn't. Not really. How could he, when *I'm* not sure what I mean? What my future looks like when my vacation time runs out.

"Oh, hey, are you on a break, or can I give you my order?" a woman about my age asks after tapping my shoulder.

I give her a, "One sec," then place my hand on Ogram's chest. Warmth and comfort and electricity race through me all at once, and when his heart beats beneath my palm, I swear mine falls in sync. "It means so much that you came to a place packed with people to spend time with me. I don't expect you to stay since I have to buzz around here like a busy bee, and it'll probably be late when I'm done, so—"

"I will wait for you."

I know he means tonight, but it feels like more. I want it to mean more.

HOPE

"Thank you *so* much," Cate says as I hand off the server's apron while she cashes me out. "I swear I'm not usually a disorganized mess. One of my longtime staff called in because her daughter came down with strep, then one of my recent hires popped her head in the door at the beginning of her shift to tell me she'd taken a shift-manager job at the hotel, effective immediately. So, I was down two servers, and yet, once you hopped on, everything was right on track, as if I were fully staffed. You're amazing."

I get a "Thank you" out past the lump in my throat. In all my years waiting tables, busting my ass, taking last-minute shifts to fill in for coworkers, my boss never appreciated me like Cate just did.

"Too bad for me that you're just in Harmony Glen on

vacation or I'd offer you a permanent job." Smiling, she removes an envelope from the drawer, closes the register, and hands me the envelope and a wad of cash. "Pay is in the envelope. Cash is your tips, my dear."

My eyes go wide as I fan the edges of the cash she gave me. Even without counting, I'm sure it's a lot more than I make on a good shift back home. "Thank you. How much is the tip out for the bartenders?"

"Zero for you. You did me a huge favor tonight, so I'm covering your tip out. *Buuut...* if you want something to do another evening, or you decide you're so happy here, you're never leaving, pop by and we'll talk."

"I'll do that," I say, and I think I mean it.

"Awesome." Cate's happy-businesswoman smile shifts to one more personal as she tilts her head toward the table in the farthest corner of the pub, and its single occupant for the past several hours. "He's never been in here before. Not once in all the years."

"That's Ogram. He's waiting for me."

"Oh, I know who he is. And *how* he his. Which is why I'm letting you know that his being here tonight, *for you*, is a big deal."

I can't resist looking over at him, and when I do, his gaze is already on me, sending all the best kinds of warmth dancing through me.

"Your personal business is none of mine," Cate says, "but I like you, and being a bit more seasoned than you, I can't help feeling a bit mother hen. So, this is just me looking out for you, but based on your verbal resume and knowing where you're from, I'm assuming you haven't dated many monsters."

"None," I confirm, tearing my attention from the big green one I can't stop thinking about. "Why?"

Gaze narrowed, her lips wiggle from side to side, then she nods, as if deciding an internal conversation with herself. "Well, the thing about trolls is that they're intense. And dedicated. Intensely dedicated, if you get my drift."

I shake my head, and she takes a deep breath and nods again, as if she's gearing up for whatever's next.

"Okay. I'm not saying they never do casual stuff," she says, nodding at the bar top where she's subtly making the universal hand movement for sex. "But that wouldn't bring your very solitary hunk of green lovin' over there out to a crowded bar to sit among dozens of people for hours. He'd just wait for you in private. His presence here, so far out of his comfort zone, is a good indicator that he sees you as his mate. As in, for life."

"I'm sure Ogram doesn't think that about me. He knows I'm only here short term. He wouldn't choose me as his mate."

"It's not a choice for trolls. It's an instinctive thing. Like love at first sight, but with the intensity dial cranked to maximum. And the way he's been looking at you all night... you're the one cranking his dial."

Hearing that, I look over my shoulder. He's still waiting. Still watching. And I still want nothing more than to finish this conversation and go to him.

"He's been part of this town since before integration,

and despite keeping to himself, he's well-liked and respected by everyone. So, if you want the same things he does, you couldn't ask for someone better to go through life with." She's wiping the bar when I face her again. Wiping for the sake of waiting for me to look at her—I'd bet my tips on it. "Just thought you should have that information if you didn't already know."

So, it's Ogram she's looking out for, not me. Or maybe both of us. "Thank you."

"Anytime, my dear," she says, winking. "Hope I see you again soon."

Nodding, I turn and cross the room. It's hours away from closing time, but the bulk of the crowd cleared out after Mari finished singing. There are empty tables now and only a handful of people dancing to jukebox music, giving me a straight line to Ogram.

"Hi," I say, dropping into the chair to his right. "I still can't believe you're here."

"I wanted to surprise you."

"Mission accomplished." I scooch my chair closer to him and weave my fingers through his. "An amazing surprise. I'm sorry I couldn't make the most of it by dancing with you. I would've loved to see your moves. What's your favorite song? I can put it on the jukebox now."

The expression of horror on his face is priceless, making it impossible *not* to dissolve into laughter.

"I don't dance," he says, once my giggles have subsided.

"Hmm, we'll see. Yesterday, you didn't come to crowded bars, either."

He doesn't dispute the point. Maybe because it's unarguable. Or maybe because he's too tired, based on the yawn he fails to contain or mask.

"You didn't have to wait around for me, and I'm happy you did, but it's late and you worked in the fields all day, so let's get you home to bed."

"Will you be joining me?"

The heat in his gaze brings memories from earlier rushing to the front of my mind. His hungry kisses. His finger sliding along the slick line of my pussy. How I would have done anything he wanted. How I wanted him to do everything.

Sitting stone still, I'm suddenly hotter than while hustling around the bar. And from the flare of his nostrils, he knows exactly where my mind is.

"Tired farmers need sleep," I say unconvincingly, even for my ears. "Will you sleep if I go home with you?"

"If you tell me not to touch you."

"Well, fat chance of that happening."

Chuckling, he lifts my hand to his lips for a soft kiss, then stands, using our joined hands to guide me up too. "Then I'll see you home and say goodnight."

"I drove here; my car is parked down the street."

"Harmony Glen is very safe, but if you'd allow me to follow in my truck, before carrying on to the farm, I would still feel better knowing you're safely inside your cabin."

"I'd like it very much if you'd see me home."

Nodding, he places one hand on my lower back, staying close by my side as we move toward the exit.

Intensely dedicated.

He sees you as his mate. As in, for life.

If you want the same things he does, you couldn't ask for someone better to go through life with.

If Cate is right, Ogram knows *I'm* the one he wants to go through life with, even though we're at the beginning of getting to know each other. Even though I'm different from him in every way. He just knows.

That's the troll way, but I'm human. We don't have an instinctive response to identify our ideal person. I've never been in love—I don't know what it's supposed to feel like. But I know what I'd want it to feel like.

Like this.

Chapter Eight

INGRAM

A late night doesn't change my body's internal clock. Even taking the morning at a leisurely Sunday pace, I'm up, fed, showered, dressed, and out the door by half past seven, ready to do some one-person jobs on my coworkers' day off. What I'm not prepared for—a dark-haired beauty in a sundress the color of summer water, sitting atop my tractor when I walk into the drive shed.

Her face lights up when I enter, dimming slightly at the sight of my work clothes. "I guess farmers don't get days off at this time of year."

"Not generally, but I can make an exception."

"I don't want your employees to be upset if they're working and I pull you away to play hooky on a sunny day."

Knowing she cares not only about me, but the relationship I have with my crew, makes my heart feel too large for my chest. Larger still because she is here, waiting and eager to spend time with me. "The farm crew has the day off, and I don't work in the market store on Sundays. Or ever, usually, but I'm still searching for someone to fill a part-time space that came open a few weeks ago."

"I'm glad you haven't filled it yet, or we wouldn't have met."

"True, and I'll be forever grateful to fate for that. But now that fate's taken care of our introduction, maybe it will see fit to send a new employee my way so I spend those two days a week with my hands in the dirt instead of pressing tiny human-sized buttons."

"If you don't like pressing tiny human-sized *buttons*, maybe I should let you get on with putting your hands in the dirt instead," she says, trying—unsuccessfully—to hide her playful smile while climbing down from the tractor.

I catch her around the waist before her second foot hits the ground, and pull her into my arms. "There is one tiny human-sized button I would love to push all day. With my fingers. My tongue."

She melts against me, the desire in her eyes mirroring my own. "Is all that button-pushing part of the *preparation?*" Her lips remain parted after that last word, the tip of her pink tongue peeking out enough to make my cock weep precum down my thigh.

Though she will never be able to take me fully into her mouth, I long to feel her tongue on my shaft. Licking me. Tasting me. "Making you come over and over, until your body is totally relaxed and wet for my cock, is part of the preparation."

"Part of it?" The faintest hint of concern flickers in her green eyes. And rightly so.

"If you want to take my cock, I'll have to stretch you with my fingers first."

"How many?" she whispers, rocking back and forth against the ridge in my pants with enough pressure to drive me mad.

"Three. Four. Maybe all of them," I say, watching her eyes open wide and her lips do the same. "If you don't want that—"

"I do. I want it all. I want it all with you."

All. She's speaking of the acts we will share. For now. And for now, that is enough.

HOPE

"Have you ridden on a tractor?" he asks.

"Never."

"Climb up."

I wait a beat to see if he's serious, and of course he is. He's Ogram. "This isn't the ride I expected you to give me."

Chuckling, he gives my ass a light pat.

Heaving an exaggerated sigh, I maneuver myself up and onto the thing for the second time. Ogram follows, lifting me effortlessly while sliding onto the seat, then settling me on his lap.

"Okay, this isn't the worst thing ever," I say, wiggling until my back is pressed tight against his broad chest.

His body shakes with silent amusement, the motion sending waves of warm tingles rippling through me. "One more adjustment will make it better." He lifts my right leg and places on the outside of his, repeats the action with my left leg, then gathers my sundress around my waist. Looking over my shoulder, he traces the edge of my lace panties, which sit just inches above the place I want his fingers most. "The evening we walked on the beach, you described skimpy underwear meant to tempt your date to remove them. Did you wear these for that purpose?"

"Yes," I say, holding my breath as he slides his hand beneath the lace.

"I look forward to removing them." He fires up the tractor with his other hand. "Until then, hold on tight, and enjoy the ride."

I gasp as the tractor lurches forward, pitching my pussy against his fingers. Two of them bracket my clit, squeezing firmly enough to make me moan and squirm. With the vibrations from the motor, the bumpy ride as we drive through a field, and Ogram's consistent, pinpoint-accuracy pressure as he rolls his fingertips around my clit, I'm helpless to do anything other than rock my against his touch. And moan. Pant. Come. "Ohhh god, oh god, yes..."

Ogram's deep rumble fills my ears. "You're not done," he says when the sensitive aftershocks hit and I try to wiggle away from his fingers. "Again. With my fingers inside you." Continuing to drive as if it's second nature, he slips one long, thick finger inside me. Swirls it around, slides it out, then enters me with two.

My pussy clenches around them, and, gripping his legs, I lean forward to take his fingers deeper, moaning when my clit presses against the mount of his palm.

"Come for me, get your cunt ready for my cock."

I suck in a breath, and his movements still.

"Are you in discomfort?"

"No, it's just, I...nobody has ever used that word with me. About me."

"I say it with passion and reverence for your body, but if it offends you, I will never speak it again."

"I...I want you to use it. With me."

"There will only ever be you." He kisses the sensitive spot where my neck meets my shoulder, slowly pumping his fingers into me while pressing his hand to my clit.

My eyes roll back in my head when a bump in the field drives his fingers deeper. "Ogram," I pant, grinding and rocking on his hand.

He answers by biting my shoulder just hard enough to send erotic heat through me. Breathing hot and fast against my skin, he finger-fucks me, curling and twisting and dragging in all the right places, pushing me into a sharp, white-hot orgasm.

When I shudder with aftershocks this time, he withdraws from my panties. His arm bands around me, pulling me against his chest as the tractor jerks to a stop.

I turn my head at the sound of his moan, and find his eyes closed, his lips sealed around his fingers. Tasting me and loving it. It's beyond hot. It's...powerful. "Does my cunt taste good?"

His dark eyes pop open, glinting with something wilder than simple arousal. "You will soon know just how delicious you are."

Simple words, but the way he says them, it's almost like a threat. Like he plans to oral me to death. I can't think of a better way to go.

"Where are we?" I ask once we're both on the ground. The crop fields are behind us. Faint track marks form a narrow path through a wooded area that appears to open into a clearing not too far ahead.

"The place I told you about, the woods where I lived before the Revelation. I keep a small barn out here as a private place for me alone. I come here when I want to feel a deep connection to my roots. My troll nature." Facing me, he takes my hand and places my palm on his chest. "If we couple today, it will trigger my rut, a deeply primal mating I have never shared with another."

"I understand why you'd want to have that experience here," I say softly, "but are you sure you want it with me?"

"I have never been more sure of anything, Hope."

This isn't just sex for him. It's a big deal. Something he's waited for, thought about. An important moment.

He sees you as his mate. As in, for life.

Nodding, maybe to him, or maybe to myself, I wrap my arms behind his neck, thread my fingers through his thick hair, and pull his head down until our foreheads and noses touch. "Share it with me."

His lips crush against mine as he sweeps me off the ground. Snug and secure in his arms, I close my eyes and open my lips, surrendering to the gentle power and passion of his kiss. I'm breathless by the time he carefully lays me out on a worn blanket atop a soft pile of hay. The ridiculously small purse I bought at the thrift store when I traded in the shoes from hell slides to the ground, reminding me of a step I'd be foolish to skip, no matter how fast he makes my heart race or how easy it is to envision a fairy-tale perfect future with him.

"The contraceptive sponges I told you about are in my purse," I say as he kneels and removes my shoes, then slides his hands up my legs, pushing my dress up with them. "I need to insert one before you insert you."

"You aren't ready to take my cock yet, and I'm going to take my time enjoying the preparation."

A shiver runs through me at his words. Another as he slides my panties down my legs.

His work-roughened hands grip my thighs and guide them open, his eyes closing as he takes a deep breath. "Gods, your scent. I have never smelled anything sweeter," he says, settling between my legs and drawing my legs onto his shoulders.

The first touch of his tongue to my clit is electric. My hips jerk upward, offering my pussy like a bowl of cherries. Because even though I'm not a virgin, this might as well be my first time. I've never had this kind of instant, intense physical response to anyone else. Never wanted someone the way I want him.

Over and over, he drags his tongue along the seam of my pussy in long passes, each one dipping deeper between my labia before ending at my clit, where he suckles and flicks until I'm at the edge, then leaves me hanging, to start again at the bottom. Just when I think I can't last another teasing pass, he stays latched on my clit, sucking and flicking while sliding two fingers inside me and curling them, twisting and tapping them.

My orgasm hits without buildup or warning, my back bowing off the blanket as I cry out. It rolls through me in waves, warmth and wetness spreading across my thighs as I buck against his face until I can barely— "Oh god, can you breathe?" I say, trying to scramble backward, but he's not having it.

Holding me in place, he lifts his head enough for me to see the sheen covering his face. And the self-satisfied smile before he licks his lips. "You will never suffocate me with your delicious cunt, though I encourage you to try."

I wouldn't have believed I'd find the word *cunt* hot, but it is when he says it to me. It flips some switch I didn't know I had. "Then get back down there." I have never told someone to eat me out. With him—easy as spreading soft butter on warm toast.

Heat flares in his dark eyes. He teases my clit with the tip of his tongue until my hips tilt toward him with a mind of their own, my body begging for more pressure, more speed. Holding my gaze, he slides fingers inside me.

More than before, and I gasp at the extra fullness. "Three?"

Nodding, he pulls my clit between his lips, his tusk teeth pressing against my labia as he doubles down on his feast.

"More," I say as he twists his fingers inside me. "Give me more." I whimper at the loss when he withdraws, moaning at the next press of fingers pushing inside me. Slowly. Carefully. But intently. A mission to prepare me for his cock. And god, I want him to succeed. Heat sears me from the inside with the stretch of his hand entering me. "Keep going," I pant when I feel his thumb knuckle press the underside of my clit.

He growls against my pussy, his tongue flicking and rolling my clit, then sucking, then, then—

My breath stops and the world goes white, like pure electricity, when he pops inside me fully. I cry out, coming in a blinding-hot rush, writhing and jerking under his mouth, my entrance circling his wrist, my pussy full to bursting with his hand inside me.

He licks me softly as I come down, easing his fingers from my still-pulsing pussy, then gently rolls me onto my hands and knees. "The first time will be easier for you this way."

The first time. He thinks my body will be able to handle more than one time after all of this?

I watch as he takes his shirt off. Opens his pants. Takes his cock out. Even after having all his fingers inside me, my eyes still feel as if they're going to pop out of my head. He said he was large, but he was being modest. Or trying not to scare me away. He's *huge.* Huge like one of those massive monster dildos online that I always assumed were for shelf effect.

"The sponge," I croak as he moves closer.

The purse looks like a child's dress-up toy in his big hand. The sponge, even more so. He examines it like a bizarre puzzle, shaking his head when I hold out my hand. "I will place it inside you. Tell me what to do."

"Gently fold it in half, then insert it as high as you can inside me, with the loop hanging down. That's for removing it later."

He gives it another dubious look before stepping in close behind me and sliding it into me so easily, I barely feel his finger.

But I feel it when his fingers coast over my skin while he pulls my dress up and off. Sparks ricochet through me then, and again as he smooths his hands over every inch of my naked body, from my hair to the soles of my feet.

"You are so beautiful," he says, stripping out of his boots and pants.

My throat goes dry at the sight of him in his fully glory. He's so big all over. Broad and thick with muscles upon muscles. And still, his cock looks like unnaturally oversized. Impossible to fit inside me, preparation or not.

To the best of my knowledge, male trolls will only experience arousal if intercourse is possible.

I sure hope he's right.

Leaning forward on my elbows tips my ass up. My thighs are still slick from the orgasms he gave me, my pussy still warm and pulsing from being fingered and fisted. Looking over my shoulder at him, I reach around and touch myself, gasping at the sensitivity, the instant urge to come.

"*Hope.*" It comes out deep and rough, his chest rising and falling fast, nostrils flaring as he strokes up and down a cock so big, it makes his hands look average in size, which they're not. Far from it. "I will not be able to stop once the rut begins."

"I'm sure," I say before he can offer me one last chance to back out. "I trust you. I want you."

Stepping behind me, he smooths his palm over my curves, then dips between my legs, sliding two fingers inside me and groaning when I push back to take them deeper. Removing his fingers, he lines his cock up with my pussy, swirling it at my entrance until he's notched between my stretched lips. "I've been waiting for you my entire life, Hope."

"No more waiting," I whisper. "I'm here now. Take me."

Chapter Nine

OGRAM

"No more waiting. I'm here now. Take me." Breathy voiced and glassy eyed, she watches me. My gaze drops from her beautiful face to her slick pink lips stretched wide around my girth. She is ready for my rut. She welcomes it, as only a mate would.

I push inside, groaning as my green cock disappears inch by inch, as her cunt—tight despite being stretched by my hand—clamps and squeezes around me.

Beneath me, her head falls to the blanket. Face in profile, eyes closed, soft panted moans leaving her parted lips, she is the most beautiful sight in the world. My mate, taking my cock. Her scent finds its way to my nose again. My fertile mate.

Heat roars to life in my chest, spreading like wildfire to my groin. My balls.

My mate. Mine.

Claim. Take. Give. Breed.

Gripping her hips, I thrust deeper. Deeper. Never withdrawing. Deeper. Deeper. Until there is no more deeper.

Balls slapping against her soft round bottom, I pound into my mate's hot cunt. Fold my body over her. Squeeze her breast. Pinch the nipple that will nurse our child.

My mate. Mine. Breed.

Her husky moaning breaks through the single-minded focus of the rut.

Sliding my hand between her legs, I growl as my fingers feel my cock stretching her cunt. She keens when I touch her clit, a garbled string of syllables and guttural sounds filling the air as I rub and roll the button until she comes. Her cunt clenches like a vise, and I pump into her, unloading deep inside her, even after her muscles relax around me.

The urge to remain embedded inside her burns as hot as the rut itself, but I fight past it. She is my mate, but not a troll. She will need to recover from taking my cock. Plus, she does not want a baby.

Rolling us onto our sides, I hold her close, stroking and kissing her everywhere I can reach, enjoying a few more seconds with my half-hard cock inside her before withdrawing carefully. "Was it too much? Are you in discomfort?" I ask when her soft gasp rises in front of me.

Angling her head to look back at me, she smiles. "No and no. I mean, it was a lot to take, but I loved taking it."

"And you took me so well, my," *mate* almost escapes, "beautiful Hope."

She beams up at me, lush roses coloring her face. "Was it what you expected? The rut, I mean. Did doing it with a human make it less than you hoped for?"

"Experiencing it with you made it perfect."

"Still sweet, even after all that." She giggles, then gasps again. "And 'all that' just made a giant puddle on your blanket."

Again, something primal flickers inside me. The urge to see the seeds of our mating, even though she has taken steps to prevent impregnation. I shift backward as she moves forward, both of our gazes going to the small pond of cum between us.

"Oh no." She cups a hand over her mouth, then points at the spill. "That's the sponge. Or, what's left of it."

Small fragments of the sponge material remain attached to the removal loop.

"You rutted the sponge out of place. No, not just that, or the whole unit would've flowed out with your bucket of cum. Is it possible your troll sperm ate right through it?" Her gaze rises, meeting mine, and her eyes go wide at what she sees on my face. "Oh my god, you're happy about this, aren't you? Why? Some sort of male pride?"

Throwing a nearby spare blanket over the mess, I move to her side, then gather her in my lap, willing my cock to behave, if only this one time. "Perhaps a small amount of male pride, but if you saw happiness in my expression, it was at the thought of having a child with you."

"You're just trying to calm me down."

"I would rather make you happy than upset, but what I said is true. As long as you want me in your life, at your side, I will be there. Pregnant or not. Child or not. Because there is nowhere else I would rather be."

"A baby is a lifetime of responsibility," she says.

"And the gift of a lifetime."

She wraps her arms around my waist, sighing against my chest. "Do you really believe in fate?"

Blanketing her with my embrace, I press a kiss to her head. "I do. How could I not when fate brought me you?" I feel her smile against my skin before she tips her head up to show it to me.

"Then I'm not going to worry about it. I'm leaving it in fate's hands."

"That's all we can do." Fate delivered for me once. I have to believe it will again. "Let's get you back to the house for a warm bath and a nap," I say when she yawns.

"Your house?"

Our house. Too soon for those words, so I nod instead, then scoop her up and make our way there.

OGRAM

The afternoon sun filters through the bedroom window, its rays on my closed eyes pulling me from sleep. Hope remains asleep beside me, unaffected by the light on her beautiful face. Carefully, I lift my head enough to see her fully. Her long dark hair fans on the pillow above her head, messy from our coupling. Her pink mouth is slightly open, quiet breaths leaving in slow, even rhythm. I lower my head to the pillow, careful not to disturb her. Somewhat careful. I cannot be a saint while she's naked in my arms.

She makes a soft *mmm* when I nuzzle my nose into her hair. Beneath the covers, her bare, warm bottom snuggles tighter against my groin.

Hard since the moment I woke, my cock grows thicker where it's nestled in the valley of her ass. Precum leaks steadily on her lower back, and I slide my hand between us, intending to wipe it away, but she catches my wrist, stopping me.

"Do you need to stretch me every time, or will you fit inside me right now?" Desire fills her sleepy voice—and her scent.

What is absent from her scent, though, is the distinct note of fertility that would trigger a rut if my cock was buried inside her, as it did this morning. Still, the possibility of causing her any type of discomfort is out of the question, no matter how much I crave her tight cunt squeezing my cock again.

"Are you not sore from earlier?" I ask, sliding my fingers over her hip and between her legs, and finding her fully slick.

"Not sore there." She moans softly as I gently circle her clit. Louder as I increase the pressure and speed. "God, yes, please, make me come, do whatever it takes so I can have your cock inside me again." She whimpers when I abandon her clit, moans when I slide two fingers into her wet cunt and flutter them against her tight walls. "Ogram, please..."

"Please what, my mate?" The words leave me, unbidden and natural. Right. When she shifts her head to look at me, I see no shock in her eyes. No fear.

"Am I?" she whispers. "Am I your mate?"

"You are." I slip my hand free of her heat and rest it low on her abdomen.

"What does that mean?"

"That you are the only one I will ever be with. That you will always be the sole keeper of my heart and soul, and I would do anything and everything within my power to make you happy, in this lifetime and beyond. I cannot change what fate decided for me, nor would I want to, even if you leave, or never love me as I do you."

"You think you love me...already?"

"I do not need to think it, I feel it. In every heartbeat, in every breath, in every sensation. You are always there. Always with me."

"That's what love feels like." Her words come out so quietly, I'm not certain she intended them for my ears.

"I said too much." With the pad of my thumb, I wipe the single tear rolling down her cheek.

"You didn't. Everything you said was perfect." Her hair moves like gentle waves under moonlight as she shakes her head. "This is happy crying."

"Like the time I didn't understand about the sponges and you laughed until you cried?"

A single, effervescent laugh leaves her smiling lips. "Not like that. This is a different kind of happy crying."

"Human emotions are much more complicated than trolls. It will take time for me to become familiar with all the nuances."

"Would forever be enough?"

Every muscle in my body tenses. "If you are once again trying to reduce the number of words spoken, I would rather you used more."

Her light giggle floats in the air between us. "I'm asking how you'd feel if I stay in Harmony Glen instead of going back. Notice I didn't say 'go home' there? That's because it hasn't felt like home in a long time, but being here does. Here, in Harmony Glen. Or here, wherever you are." Without shifting our position, she reaches up and strokes my jaw, my lips, my tooth where it lies against my cheek. "I feel you inside me too, Ogram, exactly the beautiful way you described. I love you, my mate."

Joy, full and alive in a way I have never experienced, races through me. As does need. I slide my fingers down, rolling and circling her clit until she's writhing and jerking, coming quickly and sharply against my touch. I quickly adjust myself, notching the head of my cock at her hot, wet entrance. "Take me, my mate." Claiming words. Finally.

She moans as I push inside, panting as I stretch her wider with each inch. "Yes, oh god yes, give me everything."

Gripping her hip, I thrust deeper, as deep as her body allows, holding myself still while her muscles clench around me. Smoothing my palm over her hip, I spread my fingers wide across her belly. Flat now, but not for always. Soon, she will be round with our child. I feel it as surely as she is my mate.

Her cunt softens, her body remembering it can take more, and I give it to her, sinking deeper into her heat. I bring her top leg up to rest on mine, opening her, then move my fingers to her clit as I push deeper still.

"Ogram," she moans as I seat the full length of my cock in her heat. "Is it... are you..."

"Every inch of me is inside you. Feel my balls pressed against your sweet bottom?" I ask as I thrust without retreating.

"Yes," she pants, her breath hitching as I rub her slick, engorged clit faster, harder.

"You're taking me so beautifully, my mate." My balls feel filled with fire, and all I want is to burn with her. "Your sweet cunt owns my cock, just as your heart owns mine."

She cries out, her inner muscles clamping down on me, squeezing me as she comes undone.

Buried deep, I spill for what seems like eternity while still ending far too soon. Not wanting this moment to end, I remain inside her, still half hard. "Again," I say, lazily stroking in and out and gently rubbing her clit until I coax out a long, shuddering orgasm that milks more cum from my cock.

"Will it always be like this?" she asks, turning in my arms after I grudgingly but necessarily withdraw from her heat.

I could fuck her all day, then all night. But my human mate is not made the same, and I won't risk hurting her. "If by 'this' you mean perfect, yes."

"So confident." Giggling, she kisses me softly.

"We are mated. Joined through flesh, hearts, and souls. A bond that will only grow stronger."

"You're right, that does sound perfect," she says, tracing the outline of my ear with her delicate fingertip.

The simple touch is all that's needed to return my cock to a full stand, and her eyes go wide as it presses against her belly.

"As for confidence..." I notch my cock between her legs and push inside her wet cunt, both of us moaning as I fill her in one slick, squelching stroke. "I am confident we're not leaving this bed anytime soon."

"Perfect," she whispers against my lips.

And it is.

Epilogue

HOPE

"Are you sure about this?" I ask, my finger hovering over the Pay Now button on the moving company's online invoice. "It's a lot of money that I don't know when I'll be able to pay back, and I could just as easily go back and do it myself."

Ogram sets aside the ledger he's working on—an actual paper ledger because he so vehemently dislikes the *tiny human-sized buttons* of a computer—and comes around the dining table to stand behind me. "There is no 'paying back' because it is our money," he says, massaging my shoulders. "And you shouldn't be lifting heavy objects."

"I might not be pregnant."

The rumble in his chest is equal parts amusement and male pride. Ever since his super-strong troll semen essentially ate the spermicidal sponge a couple of weeks ago, he's been quietly certain my womb is now home to a baby troll or baby human, or some mixture to be determined.

I haven't told him I think he's right. I'm afraid to get his hopes up. Or mine. Because, as much as I didn't plan this, I want it. I want it so much, I'm not sure I can wait for nature to give the thumbs up or down. The not knowing is killing me.

Leaning in, he covers my hand where it sits on the mouse and presses the left-click button. "Done. When is the delivery date?"

"I don't know. Human pregnancies are forty weeks. How long are troll pregnancies?"

His hands go tense. "The moving truck delivery of your things."

"Oh." And shit.

He pulls my chair away from the table and crouches in front of me, his dark eyes searching my face. "Are you pregnant?"

"I'm not sure. My cycle fluctuates a bit, but my period should be now-ish. I bought a pregnancy test yesterday, but I'm afraid."

"I understand. You said you aren't ready and tried to prevent it," he says, gently stroking my face. "If you don't want to be pregnant, then you won't be pregnant. There are several good doctors in Harmony Glen who will ensure your safety and well-being, and I will be by your side at every step."

"But you want a baby. You told me you wanted to get me pregnant the first night we walked on the beach."

"I want your happiness more. Always."

Every single day, he shows me how sweet he is. How beautiful and perfect our life together is going to be.

"I'm not afraid of finding out I'm pregnant. I'm afraid I won't be. And not because it's what you want. The morning it happened, I was upset for all of three seconds, just out of shock. Then you told me you want to be with me, baby or not, and I started building a picture in my mind of how that would look. I already knew I wanted a picture of me and you, but I loved the picture even more with us holding our baby. It was adorable and green like you, by the way."

Ogram drops to his knees, reaches deep into his pocket, coming out with a ring pinched between two fingers. A braided gold band with a large, square-cut emerald, flanked on two sides by diamonds surrounded by small rubies.

Taking my left hand in his, he looks deep into my eyes. "I didn't want to rush you, so I was going to wait for the right time, but there is no righter time than this. I have known since laying eyes on you that you're my mate. In every minute since, I've learned that you are who I would choose if fate hadn't. I love you. Whether we have one baby, a house full of them, or none, I want to spend forever making you happy. Will you marry me?"

"Yes," I whisper as tears roll down my face. "Yes, yes, yes." Launching myself at him doesn't so much as budge him. My big, solid, sweet, sexy troll. "I love you so much. How is it possible to love you so much?"

"That's how mates love." He kisses me then. Gently.

But not sweetly. "Get the pregnancy test," he says when we break for air. "So we can celebrate."

"What if I'm not pregnant?"

"Then we'll celebrate the opportunity to keep trying when your scent sends me into another rut."

Heat pools between my legs at the thought of him rutting me again. "I'll go pee on the stick."

Three minutes always go by in a blink—except when you're waiting for two pink lines to appear.

When I open the bathroom door, Ogram is right there waiting.

I have never been good at playing it cool. Or faking things. Or being quiet.

And now is not the time to start.

"I'm pregnant!" I squeal, throwing my arms around him. My feet leave the ground, the air whooshing out of me as he spins me around. Carefully, of course. Because I'm pregnant. "And a little disappointed," I say, trying— and failing—to keep a straight face when he sets me down. "Your troll super-sperm deprived me of more super-hot troll rutting."

Chuckling, he scoops me into his arms and heads toward our bedroom. "You'll be fertile again, my mate. Until then, we're celebrating that you're not."

Best celebration ever.

So far.

Thank you for reading *A Troll in the Hay!*

Join my mailing list and stay up to date on new releases, bonus content, sales, freebies, contests, and more. www.karladoyle.com/newsletter

Return to Harmony Glen for Ogram and Hope's wedding, where you'll get to know his brother Grush, who meets his mate—Cate from The Corner Bar—in **Rock 'n' Troll**.

Then take another visit to Harmony Glen and read Glen the tree-man's love story in **Wood You Be Vine?**

Also by Karla Doyle

Paranormal Romances:

Now You See Me (Screaming Woods)

Snake Believe (Screaming Woods)

Once Upon A Beast (Hemlock Woods)

The Beast Within (Hemlock Woods)

Mated to the Minotaur (Fate's Falls)

The Grumpy Demon's Sunshine (Fate's Falls)

A Reaper is Forever (Fate's Falls)

The Rhino's Rose (Fate's Falls)

A Dash of Demon (Fate's Falls)

Hell's Belle (Fate's Falls)

Orc-ily Ever After (Fate's Falls)

Falling for the Yeti (Fate's Falls)

A Troll in the Hay (Harmony Glen)

Rock 'n' Troll (Harmony Glen)

Wood You Be Vine? (Harmony Glen)

Contemporary Romances

Novellas:

Wedded Miss

Dad Bod Wingman (Hope Harbor)

Heart Beats (Hope Harbor)

Last Call Casanova (Hope Harbor)

Fleshing It Out (Hope Harbor)

The Deal With Love (Hope Harbor)

Doggy Style (Hope Harbor)

Resorting to Love (linked to Hope Harbor)

White Lie Christmas (linked to Hope Harbor)

King of Her Dreams (Hope Harbor)

Heart of Texas (linked to Hope Harbor)

Her Pipe Dream (Hope Harbor)

12 Days (Hope Harbor)

Puck That

Shifting Gears (Under the Hood)

Driver's Seat (Under the Hood)

Gingerbread Man (Man of the Month: Candy Cane Key)

Just in Queso (Man of the Month: Magnolia Point)

Unexpected Addition

Dating the Doubter

Contemporary Romances

Full-length Novels:

Gift Wrapped

Cup of Sugar (Close to Home #1)

Icing on the Cake (Close to Home #2)

Sweet as Candy (Close to Home #3)

Body of Work (Very Personal Training #1)

Worth the Wait (Very Personal Training #2)

Game Plan

More Than Words

Crossing the Line

Visit Karla's website for the most up-to-date list.

www.karladoyle.com

See Karla's books sorted by tropes and themes:

www.karladoyle.com/books/by-tropes/

About the Author

 A small-town girl with some big-city experience, Karla resides in South-western Ontario with her hunky husband. She studied fashion design in college and spent 20+ years working in that industry before succumbing to the writing muse. When she's not writing the sexy stories that swirl around in her head, you can find her spending time with family, hanging out with book-loving friends on Facebook, or cuddled up with a book and her adorable pets.

Karla loves hearing from readers! Connect with her online, or send her an email: karla@karladoyle.com.

Join Karla's mailing list to stay up to date on all her news. www.karladoyle.com/newsletter

facebook.com/KarlaDoyleAuthor

instagram.com/KarlaDoyleAuthor

tiktok.com/@karladoyleauthor

bookbub.com/authors/karla-doyle

goodreads.com/karlad

youtube.com/@KarlaDoyleAuthor

bsky.app/profile/karladoyleauthor.bsky.social

patreon.com/KarlaDoyleAuthor

A Troll in the Hay is part of the multi-author, shared world, Harmony Glen series. Each book is a standalone story and the books can be read in any order. Read them all and visit Harmony Glen again and again!

Get all the books:

A TROLL IN THE HAY by Karla Doyle

HISS AND TELL by Alana Khan

BIG ENOUGH TO BITE by Andie Fenichel

NEVER BEEN GARGOYLED by Ava Ross

PURRING FOR HER LION by Evangeline Priest

BREAD WITH THE ORC by Veronika Kane

HORNED TO BE WILD by Honey Phillips

FOXER UPPER by Vivienne Hart

CAN'T HELP GROWLING IN LOVE by Zoe Ashwood

TIME TO STIRRUP LOVE by AC Ruttan

THE GENIE'S WISH by Alora Quinn

REPTILE DYSFUNCTION by Alana Khan

* * *

ROCK 'N' TROLL by Karla Doyle

WOOD YOU BE VINE? by Karla Doyle

GARGOYLED AT FIRST SIGHT by Ava Ross

SATYRDAY NIGHT FEVER by Honey Phillips

SEALED WITH A KISS by Evangeline Priest

BITING BIGFOOT by Andie Fenichel

ARE YOU GONNA BE MY GHOUL? by AC Ruttan

WAITING FOR A GHOUL LIKE YOU by AC Ruttan

EMPLOYEE OF THE MOTH by Vivienne Hart

SHADES OF LOVE by Alora Quinn

SWAMP AND CIRCUMSTANCE by AC Ruttan

A KISS FOR A KRAKEN by SC Principale

BITTEN BY LOVE by Andie Fenichel